Acting Edition

STEW

by Zora Howard

D1547079

|| SAMUEL FRENCH ||

FOR PRODUCTION INQUIRIES

UNITED STATES AND CANADA
info@concordtheatricals.com
1-866-979-0447

UNITED KINGDOM AND EUROPE
licensing@concordtheatricals.co.uk
020-7054-7298

Each title is subject to availability from Concord Theatricals Corp., depending upon country of performance. Please be aware that *STEW* may not be licensed by Concord Theatricals Corp. in your territory. Professional and amateur producers should contact the nearest Concord Theatricals Corp. office or licensing partner to verify availability.

This work is published by Samuel French, an imprint of Concord Theatricals Corp.

STEW was produced by Page 73 Productions (Michael Walkup, Artistic Director; Amanda Feldman, Managing Director; and Rebecca Yaggy, Development Director) at Walkerspace in New York City opening on February 1, 2020. The performance was directed by Colette Robert, with sets by Lawrence E. Moten III, costumes by Dominique Fawn Hill, lights by Stacy Derosier, sound by Avi Amon, hair & wigs by Nikiya Mathis, and props by Caitlyn Murphy. Dramaturg Kari Olmon, Production Stage Manager Fran Acuña-Almiron. The cast was as follows:

LIL' MAMA	Kristin Dodson
NELLY	Toni Lachelle Pollitt
LILLIAN	Nikkole Salter
MAMA	Portia

CHARACTERS

LIL' MAMA – A Black girl in her pre-teens. *
NELLY – A Black girl soon to be eighteen.**
LILLIAN – A Black woman in her thirties. ***
MAMA – A mature Black woman. Don't ask her age.

*Also reads **AND A THIRD**
Also reads **ANOTHER VOICE OFFSTAGE
*** Also reads **A VOICE OFFSTAGE**

SETTING

Mt. Vernon, New York. Or a neighborhood like it.

TIME

Some time ago but not too long ago. Let's say somewhere around the
millennium. The most recent millennium.

AUTHOR'S NOTES

NOTE ON CASTING

All of the women in this play should kind of look alike.

NOTE ON STYLE

In general, the flow of conversation in this kitchen is very quick. These women do not wait to speak and are rarely ever sitting and talking; they are doing and talking as they do. They respond to each other as they damn well please – as the spirit strikes them. However, for ease of playing, the following note about layout:

1. A speech usually follows the one immediately before it except when:

    a. one character starts speaking before the other has finished, the point of interruption is marked "/".

LILLIAN. What was that sound?!

MAMA. Someone's tire/ probably!

NELLY. A FIRE?!

    b. there are multiple interruptions, which will be marked sequentially by "/", "//", "///", etc.

2. A word enclosed in brackets "[ ]" is a word suggested, but unspoken.

For all of the women who raised me.

Scene One

(*Early Saturday morning in the Tucker home. Too damn early for anyone in their right mind to be up. Though the sun has barely made herself known to the sky, it is already destined to be hot as hell.*)

(*We are in the kitchen, which is old in decor, but very well maintained. Everything pristine except an ugly brown stain on one of the walls. A tabletop radio gently beams in the background; one of those public stations that broadcast entire church services. You know the ones.*)

(*Here we find* **MAMA**, *alone. She is in her bedclothes, her head wrapped up in a satin scarf. She takes in the space before moving between several posts – clearing the counters, pulling items from the cupboard – taking her time yet moving with purpose.*)

(*She is preparing a meal.*)

(*She puts the kettle to boil for her morning tea. At the same time, tends to one of two pots cooking down on the back burners: seasoning, tasting, stirring, adjusting the fire. She is sometimes silent, sometimes humming, sometimes singing along to the radio as she moves. And when she does, it is a sweet, sweet sound:*)

MAMA.
> THIS IS THE DAY
> THIS IS THE DAY
> THAT THE LORD HAS MADE
> (THAT THE LORD HAS MADE)

>> *(Her action is deliberate and ordered. A private ritual and one she takes great pride in.)*

> I WILL REJOICE
> I WILL REJOICE
> AND BE GLAD IN IT

>> *(She is at peace, interrupted only in the slightest by a tireless dog barking somewhere in the near distance.)*

(To herself.) Imma kill that dog. I swear to God I am.

>> *(**MAMA** goes to the cupboard, pulls out her mug. Gathers her fixings. Cream. Two sugars. A little bit of cinnamon.)*

Imma kill it, Imma cut it up, and Imma cook it.

>> *(The gentle ding of a timer. The kettle steams.)*

(To the kettle.) I'm coming, I'm coming.

>> *(Then, all of a sudden:)*

>> *(A loud, popping noise from somewhere near.)*

>> *(Something shifts. **MAMA**, jumping at the sound, accidentally knocks over her cup of tea, which shatters upon hitting the floor. The dog barks madly outside.)*

(To herself.) What was that?

A VOICE OFFSTAGE. What was that—?!

MAMA. I don't know –

ANOTHER VOICE OFFSTAGE. What was that...?

MAMA. I don't know!

AND A THIRD. What was that sound?

MAMA. Don't know! Someone's tire/ probably?

A VOICE OFFSTAGE. You said a fire?!

MAMA. Jesus, Mary and Joseph. No! Someone's/ [tire]!

> *(Overwhelmed by the sudden influx of voices,* **MAMA** *tries to gather herself. She makes her way to the back window to look for the source of the sound.)*

> *(**LIL' MAMA** appears at the top landing of the staircase, hip cocked and arms crossed. She is the Drama, capital D, if you know what I mean, and not pleased to be awake. She, like* **MAMA***, is in bedclothes and a satin scarf. She makes her way down to the window.)*

LIL' MAMA. What was that?

MAMA. Oh! You startled me.

LIL' MAMA. I thought I heard –

MAMA. It was/ just someone's tire.

LIL' MAMA. It was/ outside?

MAMA. Let it alone.

LIL' MAMA. Where's Junior?

MAMA. He'll be back/ soon.

> *(**NELLY***, seventeen, also in the family, saunters into the kitchen. Bedclothes. Satin scarf. She turns off the kettle before joining the others at the window.)*

NELLY. What happened/?

I heard a// [pop] –

MAMA. Let it alone.

LIL' MAMA. //It was just someone's tire.

NELLY. But tires blow. They don't pop like that.

MAMA. Well, that's what it was.

NELLY. Where's Junior?

MAMA. He'll/ be back soon.

> *(Enter* **LILLIAN***, thirties, also in her bedclothes and satin scarf. She looks just like the* **MAMA***, but younger. She quickly surveys the kitchen before heading to the window.)*

LILLIAN. What was that?

MAMA. It was just someone's/ tire.

LILLIAN. I thought I heard –

NELLY. Someone's tire blew out.

LILLIAN. I'm not sure.

MAMA. I'm sure.

I was down here/, wasn't I?

LILLIAN. It almost sounded like [a]

And where *is* Junior?/

Should be back// by now.

MAMA. He'll be back soon.

> *(Finally finding her backbone.)*

//Doesn't matter what it was! Let it alone!

NELLY. *(Under her breath.)* … Well, you don't have to yell about/ it.

MAMA. There's too much work to be done today to be minding someone else's business.

LIL' MAMA. *(Sniffing the air.)* What's that smell?

MAMA. What smell?

LIL' MAMA. Smell like smoke.

LILLIAN. *(Sniffing the air.)* Sure does.

MAMA. I don't smell/ anything...

> *(**NELLY** crosses to the stove.)*

NELLY. It's coming from this/ pot.

MAMA. Oh my goodness!

> *(**MAMA** all of a sudden remembers the pot, which has been sizzling on the stovetop.)*

LILLIAN. That's the stew?

NELLY. *Was* the stew.

MAMA. I had my eye on it, but/ that [sound]—

LILLIAN. You wanna just add some water to it?

> *(**MAMA** doesn't respond.)*

Mama?

MAMA. What? I'm dizzy all of a sudden.

LILLIAN. Dizzy how? Like you'll fall.

MAMA. It's nothing. It comes and goes.

LILLIAN. Well sit down, Mama.

MAMA. I said I'm/ fine.

I'm hot is all.

LILLIAN. *(To **LIL' MAMA**.)* Put some water in a bowl, pour it in that pot.

(*To* MAMA.)

Do you remember where you are?

MAMA. What?/ I said it's nothing. Get out my face, Lillian.

LIL' MAMA. (*To* LILLIAN.) Poured it.

LILLIAN. Stir.

LIL' MAMA. (*As she stirs.*) Sure does smell. Phew!

MAMA. (*Re the stew.*) It's ruined.

LILLIAN. (*Pacifying.*) It's not ruined.

MAMA. (*Near tears.*) It's ruined.

LILLIAN. It'll taste smokey is all –

> (*Without any warning,* MAMA *scoops up the problem pot and dumps the contents in the trash. She is moving swiftly now.*)

MAMA!

MAMA. (*To* NELLY.) Come take this trash to the basement. It's stinking up the house.

> (NELLY *does.*)

LILLIAN. Mama, that's a waste!

MAMA. Don't I know it!

LILLIAN. It would've been fine.

MAMA. We're losing half the morning.

> (MAMA *starts moving around the kitchen in search of something.* LILLIAN *sees the shattered coffee cup on the floor.*)

LILLIAN. (*Re the cup.*) This fell?

> (MAMA *sees the shattered coffee cup as well. Stares.*)

MAMA. Obviously it fell.

It slipped when—just now/ when…

LILLIAN. Lil' Mama, go get the broom and come clean this up.

LIL' MAMA. Where's the broom?

LILLIAN. In the/ back.

(**LIL' MAMA** *goes in search of the broom.*)

MAMA. It's fine. I can do it/ myself.

LILLIAN. Can you just sit down for a second?

MAMA. I don't have time to sit down. Didn't I say we got today to get this done? I said it a thousand times. What'd I say? I said please don't nobody make no plans on this one day of the year because on this one day of the year, it is very important/ that I –

LILLIAN. You're getting yourself worked/ up.

MAMA. *(Continuing from above.)* And lo and behold, here comes that one day of the year just like I said it would and it's almost noon and we've got nothing to show for it.

NELLY. It's not even seven.

MAMA. Don't tell me the time. I didn't ask you the time, don't tell me the/ time.

LILLIAN. It's gonna get done. It always/ does.

MAMA. Where's my purse?

LILLIAN. *(Sighing.)* Which purse?

MAMA. The uh – uh –

NELLY. Where'd you leave it?

MAMA. *(Snappy.)* Here somewhere.

NELLY. Here where?

MAMA. *(Snappy.)* Well, if I knew!

    (LIL' MAMA is back, empty-handed.)

LIL' MAMA. *(Re the broom.)* It's not in the/ back.

LILLIAN. *(To LIL' MAMA.)* Go upstairs and see if you see her purse somewhere.

LIL' MAMA. What it look like?

MAMA. *(Snappy.)* The black one!

LIL' MAMA. *(To LILLIAN.)* How'm supposed to know what her purse look like?

LILLIAN. Go.

    (LIL' MAMA stomps up the stairs.)

NELLY. Did you leave it downstairs?

MAMA. I carry it all the time. I just had it, I –

LILLIAN. We'll find it. Now, can you tell me about the/ [spells]?

NELLY. *(To MAMA.)* Ma, did you leave it downstairs?

MAMA. *(To herself, as she searches.)* There's no way this will be done in time –

LILLIAN. Ma, would you please sit down? We need to talk about these/ [spells]

MAMA. No, I *need* my purse.

LILLIAN. You need it right this moment?

MAMA. What kind of question is that? Yes, I need it right this moment. Would I be looking for it right this moment if I didn't need it right/ this –

NELLY. *(Holding up a black leather purse.)* Purse.

MAMA. Hand me my cigarettes out of there.

LILLIAN. Seriously?

MAMA. Well, I don't want her to make believe hand me them.

LILLIAN. I thought we were trying to quit.

MAMA. Don't patronize me.

LILLIAN. The doctor says/ that we should start –

MAMA. a lot of things. The doctor says a lot of things and I listen to most.

> (*To* NELLY.)

Give me them cigarettes. I'm not asking.

> (LILLIAN *looks to* NELLY *for support.*)

NELLY. (*To* LILLIAN.) She'll just go out and buy some if I don't.

> (NELLY *hands* MAMA *the cigarettes.*)

MAMA. It's just one a day now. I'm only doing one a day now.

> (*As she exits.*)

Put the water to boil. Please. Someone.

> (MAMA *exits to elsewhere in the house.* LILLIAN *turns on* NELLY.)

LILLIAN. How long has that been happening?

NELLY. The smoking?

LILLIAN. The "coming and going".

NELLY. I don't know.

LILLIAN. You don't know?

NELLY. A while?

LILLIAN. That's the best you can do? A while?

NELLY. Can you do better?

LILLIAN. Have you asked her about it?

NELLY. Of course I've asked her about it.

LILLIAN. And she says?

NELLY. Same thing she always says. Mind my business. And that's exactly what I do.

LILLIAN. It is our business.

NELLY. I don't want it. You can have it.

It's alllll yours.

LILLIAN. You don't get to choose.

NELLY. Watch me.

>   (NELLY *turns for the stairs.*)

LILLIAN. Uh uh. Where do you think you're going?

NELLY. Back to bed. I'm tired.

LILLIAN. Why you so tired?

NELLY. Mind your business.

LILLIAN. Don't have nothing to do with that boy Whatshisname, does it?

NELLY. You know his name. And he ain't no boy.

LILLIAN. He ain't a/ boy?

>   (NELLY *cannot resist. She swivels on a dime.*
>   *During the following,* LILLIAN *prepares the*
>   *pot to restart the stew.*)

NELLY. He's a grown ass MAN, thank you very much. He ride his own bike, he basically got his own place/ and he –

LILLIAN. Place got room for two?

NELLY. Has plenty of room, actually.

LILLIAN. Sure hope so cause that's right where you'll be when she find out you been sneaking around fucking/ some boy.

NELLY. We don't fuck.

LILLIAN. HA!

NELLY. We make love.

LILLIAN. … That's even funnier than the last thing you said.

NELLY. Whatever. Just don't tell her.

> (**LILLIAN** *scoffs.*)

Please?

LILLIAN. Then come on snap these beans so I can start the stew.

> (*Yelling up the stairs.*)

Lil' Mama!

NELLY. (*Referring to* **MAMA**.) She does the stew.

LILLIAN. She needs to be off of her feet.

> (*Again yelling up the stairs.*)

LIL' MAMA.

NELLY. As long as she got feet you know damn well she not gonna let you "do the stew."

LILLIAN. (*Defensive.*) I can do the stew.

NELLY. Not if we intend for people to eat it.

LILLIAN. Whatever.

NELLY. …and live.

LILLIAN. (*Again yelling up the stairs.*) LIL' MAMA!!

LIL' MAMA. (*Off.*) I'M COMING!!

(**NELLY** *starts up the stairs.* **MAMA** *reenters the kitchen.*)

LILLIAN. I don't know who she think she is yelling up the house/ like that.

MAMA. I don't know who you think you are yelling up the house like that.

LILLIAN. Yes, Mama.

MAMA. *(Catching* **NELLY.***)* Where you think you going?

NELLY. Back to bed?

MAMA. Oh, no you're not!

NELLY. *(Whining.)* But, Mama, I'm tired.

MAMA. You know who else was tired?

LILLIAN. Here we go.

MAMA. Jesus was tired. He was tired when he walked all that way to Calvary after being flogged and beaten and spat on and He was tired sitting up there on that cross for six hours bleeding out His hands and feet/ and legs and eyeballs –

NELLY. Oh my God.

MAMA. Yes, the remarkable thing about it is that He still *is* your God even though you spite Him so.

LILLIAN. *(Facetious.)* How'd you sleep, Mama?

MAMA. What d'you mean how'd I sleep? I slept fine.

LILLIAN. I'm just tryna figure out do you wake up like this every morning?

MAMA. Careful.

LILLIAN. Just making conversation.

MAMA. I don't need you to make conversation. I need you to make these greens.

LILLIAN. Yes, Mama.

MAMA. *(Reading off a Post-it Note on the fridge.)* Who's Terry?

LILLIAN. What?

MAMA. Say "Terry called for Lillian."

> (LILLIAN *takes the post-it from* MAMA. *Studies it longer than it takes to read.)*

NELLY. Called here.

LILLIAN. He called here?

NELLY. That's what I said.

LILLIAN. Oh.

Probably checking in on this project. I said I would/ call.

MAMA. Who's Terry?

LILLIAN. One of the teachers at the school, remember?

MAMA. *(Defensive.)* Of course, I remember.

> (MAMA *almost steps in the mess of the shattered tea cup.)*

What is – Why is this mess still here?

Do I have to do every little thing in this house myself?

> *(To* NELLY.*)*

Come over here clean this up now.

> (NELLY *does as she's told, picking up the larger pieces of porcelain off the floor and throwing them in the trash.)*

LILLIAN. Lil' Mama is doing that—

> *(Calling up the stairs.)*

LIL' MAMA!

MAMA. Please with the yelling today!

LILLIAN. Go lay down, Mama.

MAMA. I will NOT *lie* down.

LILLIAN. I'm just tryna help, Mama. Jesus.

MAMA. Don't take the Lord's name in vain in my house, Lillian.

I don't care how old you are.

LILLIAN. Yes,/ Mama.

LIL' MAMA. *(To* **LILLIAN.***)* Yes, Mama?

> *(***LIL' MAMA** *again at the top of the stairs. Arms crossed. Hips cocked.)*

LILLIAN. *(Seeing* **LIL' MAMA.***)* You hear me calling you all those times?

LIL' MAMA. *(Yes she did.)* No, Mama, I didn't hear you calling all/ them times.

LILLIAN. Didn't I tell you to come sweep up this mess?

LIL' MAMA. And then you told me to go find her purse!

MAMA. I said it's fine. Nelly is –

> *(Upon seeing* **NELLY.***)*

Little girl, what are you doing?!

NELLY. You said clean it up. I'm cleaning it up!

MAMA. If you don't go get the doggone broom and act like you have some sense.

NELLY. You didn't specify!

LILLIAN. *(To* **LIL' MAMA.***)* Go up there wash your face brush your teeth and come on now. We have work to do.

LIL' MAMA. Awwww, Mama. Can I get thirty more minutes?

MAMA. Let the girl sleep thirty more minutes.

NELLY. Can I get thirty more minutes?

MAMA. No.

NELLY. Awww, Mama!

LILLIAN. *(To* **LIL' MAMA.***)* Quickly. And you better not get back in that bed.

> (**LIL' MAMA** *exits back up the stairs in fierce albeit silent protest.* **NELLY** *exits elsewhere for the broom.* **MAMA** *sorts through a tray of vegetables on the counter.)*

MAMA. Are these washed?

LILLIAN. Mama, you should rest.

MAMA. *(Ignoring.)* Are these washed?

LILLIAN. I was just getting to it.

MAMA. Well, turn off the fire then, Lillian. These needed to be put on now.

LILLIAN. That's what I'm doing, Mama.

MAMA. No, that's what you about to do. Cause if you were doing it, it'd be done.

LILLIAN. Okay, okay.

MAMA. I don't like being late.

LILLIAN. *(Under her breath.)* You always late.

MAMA. *(She heard her.)* What?

LILLIAN. Noth/ing.

MAMA. Don't tell me I'm always late. I'm always held up is what it is. Gonna tell me I'm/ always late.

LILLIAN. You right.

MAMA. Did you get the vinegar?

LILLIAN. *(She didn't.)* Shoot!

MAMA. *(More dramatic than it needs to be.)* You didn't get the vinegar?

LILLIAN. I'll send Lil' Mama. It's fine.

> *(Up the stairs.)*

LIL' MAMA!

MAMA. Would someone please tell me how HOW am I to start the stew with half the ingredients still at the store!

LILLIAN. It's not that big of a deal, Mama, shit.

> *(Up the stairs.)*

LIL' MAMA!

MAMA. Watch your mouth.

LILLIAN. Fine!

> *(Up the stairs.)*

LIL' MAMA!

LIL' MAMA. I SAID I'M COMING!!!!

MAMA. She needs to stay down here and help.

> *(Calling off.)*

NELLY!

LILLIAN. Junior will help. He should be here soon.

MAMA. There's no way this will all get done.

LILLIAN. He'll be back by the time we heading to the church.

I let him spend the night at that little boy Nicodemus' house, remember?

MAMA. *Nicodemus?*

LILLIAN. Yes, Nicodemus.

MAMA. His mama named him Nicodemus?

LILLIAN. *(Shrugs.)* It's in the Bible.

MAMA. It's a lotta names in the Bible, Lillian.

LILLIAN. Well, that's they business.

MAMA. Simon, Andrew, James, Paul/, Matthew –

LILLIAN. Alana's prerogative, I guess.

MAMA. Alana?

LILLIAN. Yes, his mother, Alana.

MAMA. You talking bout little Nico, Alana's son?

LILLIAN. Yes...

MAMA. Little Nico Alana Miss Gerald sing bass in the choir niece's son?

LILLIAN. Miss Gerald sing bass in the choir?

MAMA. Choir Director say if we have to hear her, better to hear her where she can't hardly produce no sound.

LILLIAN. Oh. Well, yes. That Nico.

MAMA. *(Outraged.)* UH-UH!!

LILLIAN. *(Startled by* **MAMA***'s outburst.)* What what what, Mama?!

MAMA. *(Grave.)* Them people dirty.

LILLIAN. Oh, Mama!

MAMA. Miss Gerald opened her purse in practice other day offered me a mint. I swear a whole army of roaches came marching out. Didn't scurry. Just came out marching like someone owed them money. Them roaches had purpose.

LILLIAN. *(This is ridiculous.)* ... What?

MAMA. Dirty people, dirty habits.

LILLIAN. Oh, would you quit!

(*Up the stairs.*)

LIL' MAMA!

MAMA. I work very hard, *very* hard, to keep this house clean.

(*Off.*)

NELLY, BRING THAT BROOM!

LILLIAN. Well, I like the little boy. He's a good influence.

MAMA. What's that mean?

LILLIAN. Rather Junior running around outside with him than getting into who knows what by himself.

MAMA. That's the problem. He don't need to be running around no how.

LILLIAN. Boys supposed to run around outside, Mama.

They supposed to be out in the world.

(*Up the stairs.*)

LIL' MA/ –

(**LIL' MAMA** *appears at the top of the stairs.*)

LIL' MAMA. (*Exasperated.*) Yes, Mama?

LILLIAN. (*To* **LIL' MAMA.**) Didn't I say go up there and brush your teeth and come down here to help?

LIL' MAMA. I brushed my teeth!

MAMA. Boys supposed to stay close to home. Where you can see them, if you asked me.

LILLIAN. (*Under her breath.*) If I asked you.

(To **LIL' MAMA**.*)*

Come here let me smell.

MAMA. Whole heap a trouble/ "out in the world" waiting to be got into.

LIL' MAMA. *(To* **LILLIAN**.*) Seriously?*

LILLIAN. Seriously.

> *(Again,* **LIL' MAMA** *begrudgingly descends the stairs and crosses to* **LILLIAN**.*)*

MAMA. Keep the boys close. Keep the girls/ closer.

LILLIAN. *(To* **LIL' MAMA**.*)* Closer.

> *(Having descended,* **LIL' MAMA** *breathes heavily in* **LILLIAN**'*s face.* **LILLIAN** *reacts dramatically.)*

LILLIAN. What'd you brush with? Spit?

If you don't go brush your teeth and be down here in thirty seconds.

I'm not playing with you.

MAMA. *(To herself, but for others to hear.)* We don't have the vinegar, so I can't do/ the greens.

And if I can't do the greens –

> *(***LIL' MAMA** *starts stomping back up the stairs. Before she's gone completely:)*

LILLIAN. *(In response to* **MAMA**'*s monologuing.)* And Lil' Mama!

> *(***LIL' MAMA** *starts back down the stairs.)*

LIL' MAMA. *(Strained.) Yes,* Mama.

LILLIAN. While you up there look in my purse and get ten dollars so you can run to the store and get me some vinegar.

MAMA. No, Imma just figure something else out, I guess.

LIL' MAMA. *(To* LILLIAN.*)* But Mama, I have things to do!

MAMA. *(Re* LIL' MAMA.*)* Because it's always something.

We'll need more neck bone/ now too.

LILLIAN. *(To* MAMA.*)* They don't have neck bone at the corner store, Mama.

MAMA. I know they don't have neck bone at the corner store, Lillian.

LILLIAN. It's already three packs in the pot.

MAMA. Plus what we lost earlier.

NELLY. I can go.

MAMA. *(To* NELLY.*)* You can finish doing what you're doing.

(Back to LILLIAN.*)*

It's seven pounds of string beans, Lillian.

LILLIAN. Seven pounds of – How many people we cooking for, Mama?

MAMA. Well, I'm hoping the stew by itself can/ stretch, so that with everything we can feed 'bout fifty// people.

NELLY. *(To* LIL' MAMA, *re sweeping.)* You/ do this, I'll go to the store.

LILLIAN. *(Incredulous.)* //Fifty people?!

MAMA. *(To* NELLY *and* LIL' MAMA.*)* No one is going to the store.

(Back to LILLIAN.*)*

Forty-five, fifty, yeah.

LILLIAN. Mama!

MAMA. What? When people sit that long, they expect to eat, Lillian.

LILLIAN. *(Aware of* LIL' MAMA.*)* Mama, I don't have money to feed no fifty people.

LIL' MAMA. Can y'all just call me when y'all made a decision?

LILLIAN. *(A very real threat.)* I'm 'bout to make a decision.

> (LIL' MAMA *sucks her teeth. Crosses to the fridge to rummage.)*

MAMA. J.R. didn't give you no cash before you left?

LILLIAN. No,/ he—

MAMA. No?

LILLIAN. He's not – he don't have it right now.

MAMA. What's that mean?

LILLIAN. We're just...being careful, you know.

MAMA. I *don't* know is why I'm asking.

LILLIAN. He's started this new job in Warfield and things are slow right now, but it's fine.

MAMA. Well, why didn't you tell me?

LILLIAN. Tell you what?

MAMA. That you needed money? I could scrounge something up.

LILLIAN. *(Aware of the room.)* Mama, that's not – I don't need money.

> *(To* LIL' MAMA.*)*

Go upstairs and look in either my pants pocket or my jacket pocket and bring me the fifty dollar bill that's in there...or my purse.

LIL' MAMA. Where's your purse?//

LILLIAN. Next to the bed. Or by the toilet. Or in the closet
or on top of the dresser. Or at the foot of the bed –

MAMA. //It's fine, Lillian.

> *(To* NELLY.*)*

Go downstairs and look in either the big freezer or the
mini one and see if you see some neck bone in there.
Should be in the back. Or to the left/. Or in the door.
And check the date.

LILLIAN. Mama, please. I said I got it.

> *(To* LIL' MAMA.*)*

Go.

MAMA. *(To* NELLY.*)* Go.

> *(*NELLY *and* LIL' MAMA *exit.* MAMA *finds the
> butter beans, opens the packet onto a tray,
> starts to inspect for rocks. The pace in the
> kitchen eases up just a hair.)*

So when's he coming?

LILLIAN. When's who coming?

MAMA. J.R.

LILLIAN. I just told you, Mama. He has business in
Warfield.

MAMA. What's that mean?

LILLIAN. Warfield's far.

MAMA. What's that mean?

LILLIAN. It's a long drive and – I'm not saying he's not
coming, but it's/ possible he

MAMA. *(And here come the dramatics.)* He's not coming?

LIL' MAMA. *(Off.)* MAMA!

MAMA. When were you gonna tell me he wasn't coming?

LILLIAN. Well, there was always a/ chance

MAMA. You know, I don't ask for much.

> *(For the most part,* **MAMA** *will speak continuously throughout the following.)*

LIL' MAMA. *(Off.)* MAMA, IT'S NOT HERE!

MAMA. I have one day. One day out of three hundred and sixty five that I ask everyone to show up. One day.

LIL' MAMA. *(Off.)* MAMA!

LILLIAN. *(Up the stairs.)* DID YOU LOOK IN THE CLOSET?

MAMA. and all these years you never show and I don't bother you/ about it

LILLIAN. Oh, you don't bother me/ about it?

LIL' MAMA. *(Off.)* AND NEXT TO THE BED AND BY THE TOILET AND IN THE CLOSET AND ON TOP OF THE DRESSER AND AT THE FOOT/ OF THE BED!

LILLIAN. *(Up the stairs.)* LOOK IN MY BLUE PANTS IN THE HAMPER!

MAMA. *(Ignoring* **LILLIAN.***)* and then finally you do show up, out of the blue, and I'm so excited to see you – although you could've given me some warning – and I get so excited. Everyone is going to be here, everyone together like it used to be. I don't have to do it all by myself. So, I'm preparing like everyone was gonna be here cause that's what you said and that's what I'm expecting and that's what everyone is expecting/. Because it's a lot of work to be done around here, you know. There's that hole in my bedroom where he put the AC last time and that left a draft and I been talking about that draft since God// knows when and the only reason I'm even holding on to this house is for everyone to have somewhere to stay when they show up here because it sure ain't doing nothing for my health///.

LILLIAN.   I can't be worried about what everyone is expecting, Mama.

// I can deal with the draft, but –

LIL' MAMA. *(Off.)* THEY NOT IN THE HAMPER!

LILLIAN. *(Trying to be delicate.)* /// Well, Mama, maybe we need to talk about that.

The doctor said/ that –

LIL' MAMA. *(Off.)* MA, THEY NOT IN THE HAMPER!

LILLIAN. *(Exasperated.)* The doctor said/ that –

MAMA. Lillian, would you please stop talking to me about what the doctor said like I wasn't standing there when he was saying it!

LILLIAN. *(Getting a little worked up now.)* Well, were you listening?!

MAMA. *(Raising her voice.)* I'm not raising my voice at you, don't raise your voice at me, Lillian.

Now, I been practically begging y'all to come and spend some time here every year since—and it took "what the doctor said?" to get you to show up at all and it's only cause you feel guilty/

LILLIAN. That's not/ even –

LIL' MAMA. *(Off.)* EXCUSE ME, THEY NOT IN THE HAMPER!

MAMA. and that's good for your behind cause it shouldn't be so doggone hard for y'all to come around every once in a while and check in on me and say, "Hey, you need something done round here" or, "I heard you got a solo in the choir, Mama, and I wanna come support cause I know that's very important/ to you."

LILLIAN. It's just not feasible with everything going on and J.R. barely around and we having a hard time with that already –

LIL' MAMA. *(Off.)* I ONLY SEE BLACK ONES IN THE HAMPER!

MAMA. What's that mean?

LILLIAN. What's what mean?

MAMA. "Having a hard time"?

LILLIAN. We're just—we're just having a hard time, but we're fine.

LIL' MAMA. *(Off.)* HELLO!

LILLIAN. *(Losing her shit now.)* WELL DID YOU *LOOK* IN THE BLACK ONES?!

MAMA. Well, how long y'all been having a hard time?

LILLIAN. It doesn't, I'm not gonna – God, Mama... Listen, I just feel that sometimes at the church they take advantage of you and it's really too much/ to be –

MAMA. Well, sometimes it's nice to have someone take some advantage of you.

LILLIAN. It's nice to have someone take advantage of you?

MAMA. *(Taking a breath as to explain.)* Get some use out of you is what I'm saying, Lillian. I like cooking for people. So, yes, it's nice to cook for more than one every once in a while since I've not had the privilege of cooking/ for my

LILLIAN. Aww, would you lay off with/ the [guilt trip]

MAMA. You know, I'm getting old and I don't know how many more years I got left and with daddy gone, I'm thinking of following right behind him.

LILLIAN. Oh, Mama, please!

MAMA. Please, what?

LILLIAN. Are you dying?

MAMA. Well, it's certainly the direction in which I am heading.

LILLIAN. Are you done?

MAMA. Should've been done a long time ago way I been wasting away in this house waiting on you to come/ see me –

LILLIAN. Aww, Mama, it wouldn't be so hard/ to be here if I didn't expect to be –

MAMA. So hard? Is it *so hard*?

LILLIAN. I'm not doing this with you.

MAMA. Oh, you not doing it with me, but I did it with you. I did it with you and then that man and them children in my house using up my heat and my gas and electricity and I didn't say nothing about it because that's what we do and we do it because we expect it to be done back for us one day when we old and tired and clinging to life.

> (**LILLIAN** *starts laughing somewhere in the middle of this. This is her surrender. She is no match for* **MAMA.**)

LIL' MAMA. *(Off.)* MAMA IT'S NOT UP HERE!

MAMA. What? What is so funny, Lillian? Huh, what is so doggone funny?

LIL' MAMA. *(Off.)* IT'S NOT UP HERE, MAMA!

> (*Somehow,* **MAMA** *starts laughing too. Armistice.* **LILLIAN** *and* **MAMA** *laugh together.*)

MAMA. I don't know why you laughing.

LILLIAN. You laughing!

MAMA. *(Laughing.)* I'm not laughing.

> *(The laughing subsides. They return to the needs of the kitchen. Beat.)*

LILLIAN. You're sick, Mama.

MAMA. Sick of my ungrateful children, yes.

> *(No, no. This is different. Quieter.)*

LILLIAN. You're sick.

> *(Pause.)*

MAMA. It comes and goes.

Most it is, I'm talking and all the words come out in order except one or two.

I know all the words. I just don't remember the order.

Time gets a little...tricky. Or, it gets trickier with time.

Whatever they say.

Just gotta pay more attention.

And, hell, if it means I get everyone together because of it, I'm not too mad.

Seem like somebody gotta die for us to all get together in one room.

LILLIAN. Alright, alright, Mama. Nobody's dying.

MAMA. You'll talk to J.R.?

LILLIAN. ... I'll talk to him.

Scene Two

(Later in the Tucker kitchen.)

(All of the women tending to business elsewhere save **NELLY**, *who was left to watch over the few items currently cooking down on the stove. She, however, is otherwise occupied. On the phone:)*

NELLY. *(On the phone.)* Yeah?

Yeah?

Yeahhhhhhh?

(She giggles sillily.)

Boy, you so stupid.

Yeah.

Yeahhhhh.

Stupid.

*(***LIL' MAMA*** enters. She cannot help but to eavesdrop on* **NELLY**'*s conversation, who, though having slightly adjusted her volume level upon* **LIL' MAMA**'*s entrance, is still quite animated.* **LIL' MAMA**, *not shy about making audible sounds of disgust in response, mimics* **NELLY**'*s body language behind her back. She's quite good at this.)*

Oh, so what, you don't miss me?

No?

Not even a lil' bit?

Shut up, you know you miss me.

Yeahhhhh.

> (*More giggling.*)

No, you hang up.

You hang up.

You hang up.

LIL' MAMA. How about *you* hang up?

> (**NELLY** *shoots* **LIL' MAMA** *an evil look.*)

NELLY. (*To* **LIL' MAMA.**) Shut up.

> (*Back to phone.*)

No, not you, silly!

But, yeah, I gotta go.

I'll call you later.

I promise.

> (**NELLY** *hangs up the phone. The giddiness we witnessed on the phone quickly fades away. She returns to the needs of the kitchen.* **LIL' MAMA** *watches her silently, obviously waiting for some kind of engagement.*)

(*Finally.*) Yes, Lil' Mama?

LIL' MAMA. Who was that?

NELLY. Mind your business.

LIL' MAMA. Come on, I won't tell.

NELLY. ...

LIL' MAMA. That was your boyyyyyyyyyyyfriend?

NELLY. ...

LIL' MAMA. huh?

　　...

　　Huh?

　　... HUH?

NELLY. No, that wasn't my boyfriend.

　　...

　　That was my *man*.

LIL' MAMA. What's the difference?

NELLY. A boyfriend is temporary.

　　A man is forever.

LIL' MAMA. *Forever?* ... that sounds like a lonnnnng time.

NELLY. You wouldn't understand.

　　It's grown folks business.

LIL' MAMA. ... But you not grown.

NELLY. Yes. I am.

LIL' MAMA. ... No. You not.

NELLY. Am.

LIL' MAMA. Not.

NELLY. Am.

LIL' MAMA. Not.

NELLY. Am! —I'm not doing this with you.

　　　　(Pause. LIL' MAMA *considers.)*

LIL' MAMA. What's in between?

NELLY. What?

LIL' MAMA. If a boyfriend is temporary and a man is forever, what's in between?

NELLY. Ain't no in between. They all temporary 'til you find you one forever.

LIL' MAMA. ... I don't get it.

NELLY. Look, when you don't have no boyfriend, which you don't, and you don't have no man, which you don't, it's just you in the between.

LIL' MAMA. Me.

NELLY. Yeah, you. Just you by yourself, waiting 'til it ain't temporary no more. Waiting 'til it's forever.

LIL' MAMA. Oh.

NELLY. If you're lucky, you find it young. Like me. Better that way.

LIL' MAMA. Why?

NELLY. So you don't have to wait so long. Better to find it young.

LIL' MAMA. You sure it's better?

NELLY. What?

(**LILLIAN** *enters from upstairs.*)

LILLIAN. *(To* **LIL' MAMA.***)* Brush your teeth?

LIL' MAMA. Brushed my teeth.

LILLIAN. Wash your hands.

LIL' MAMA. Washed my hands.

LILLIAN. Then wash these.

(**LILLIAN** *hands* **LIL' MAMA** *a bag of string beans.* **LIL' MAMA** *begins to wash.*)

Who called?

NELLY. No one for/ you.

LIL' MAMA. Her boyfriend.

NELLY. Lil' Mama!

LIL' MAMA. I mean her man!

LILLIAN. Oh, her man, huh?

And what he say?

NELLY. He said mind your business.

LILLIAN. As long as you minding yours.

(**NELLY** *sucks her teeth.*)

LIL' MAMA. What we making?

LILLIAN. Food.

LIL' MAMA. What kind of food?

LILLIAN. The kind you eat.

LIL' MAMA. What kind you eat?

LILLIAN. The kind that's good.

LIL' MAMA. What for?

NELLY. *Jesus.*

LIL' MAMA. For Jesus?

LILLIAN. *(To* **LIL' MAMA.***)* "*What for*"?

LIL' MAMA. What we making it/ for?

LILLIAN. *(A sharp correction.)* "Why are we making it."
Stop talking like you're on the street.

(*Relenting.*)

A function.

LIL' MAMA. A function?

LILLIAN. *(Sighing.)* At the church. A very important function at the church.

LIL' MAMA. But it's not even Sunday.

NELLY. It's always Sunday in this house.

LILLIAN. *(To* LIL' MAMA.*)* Wash.

LIL' MAMA. Why Junior don't have to help?

NELLY. Yes, why doesn't Junior have to help?

LILLIAN. He's at his friend Nicodemus' house.

LIL' MAMA. *(Incredulous.) Nicodemus?*

NELLY. You mean little Nico, Alana's son?

LILLIAN. *(Exasperated.)* Yes, little Nico Alana Miss Gerald sing bass in the choir niece's son.

NELLY. *(A discovery.)* Miss Gerald sing bass in the choir?

LILLIAN. Apparently.

NELLY. *(Dripping with judgment.)* Mmm mmm mmm.

LILLIAN. *(For God's sake.)* They're nice people.

NELLY. Nice and dirty.

LILLIAN. You sound just like her.

(LIL' MAMA *raises her hand.)*

Yes, Lil' Mama.

LIL' MAMA. I don't think it's fair Junior get to play while I have to stay here and help.

LILLIAN. Is that so?

LIL' MAMA. If anyone should have to help, it's Junior.

LILLIAN. And why's that?

LIL' MAMA. He's younger! And I have things to do.

LILLIAN. What things?

LIL' MAMA. Important things.

NELLY. Yeah, like what?

LIL' MAMA. *(Ignoring **NELLY**.)* If Junior don't have to help, I shouldn't have to help either.

NELLY. She do gotta point.

LILLIAN. *(Ignoring **NELLY**.)* Go in that cabinet, get the red bowl and start snapping. Even pieces. And don't mix the ends back in there.

LIL' MAMA. *(Under her breath.)* Tyrant.

LILLIAN. It's good for you to be learning how to do this, Lil' Mama.

I had to learn.

She had to learn.

LIL' MAMA. Why?

LILLIAN. It's a very useful skill.

NELLY. *(Scoffs.)* You sound just like her.

LIL' MAMA. Why?

NELLY/LILLIAN. (**NELLY** *mocking.)* A woman should know how to cook.

LIL' MAMA. Why?

LILLIAN. *(Getting irritated.)* Because one day you'll have people to cook for and you'll need to know.

LIL' MAMA. Why?

LILLIAN. Because it's important.

LIL' MAMA. Why?

LILLIAN. *(Through.)* You know what? Y is a crooked letter.

    (Beat.)

It's important to know how to look after someone.

And it's more important to know how to look after yourself.

> (**LIL' MAMA** *contemplates this.*)

LIL' MAMA. ... Junior don't need to know how to look after hisself?

LILLIAN. *(A correction.) Himself.* And yes... it's just— *(Stumped.)*

He does need to know, but in... other ways.

LIL' MAMA. *(A challenge.)* Other ways?

LILLIAN. *(A directive.)* Snap.

> (**LIL' MAMA** *goes in the cabinet, finds the bowl and starts snapping.*)

LIL' MAMA. When's daddy coming?

NELLY. Do you stop asking questions?

LILLIAN. *(To* **LIL' MAMA.***)* Why are you asking me that?

LIL' MAMA. I'm just asking.

LILLIAN. Just asking?

NELLY. Girl can't ask when her daddy coming?

LILLIAN. *(Ignoring* **NELLY.***)* Lil' Mama?

LIL' MAMA. He's helping me.

LILLIAN. Helping you with what?

LIL' MAMA. Things.

NELLY. You're mumbling.

LILLIAN. Okay, enough. What are these "things"?

LIL' MAMA. *(Mumbling.)* ... I've got an audition.

NELLY. You're mumbling.

LILLIAN. You what?

NELLY. She said she has an audition.

> (**LIL' MAMA** *cuts her eyes at* **NELLY.**)

LILLIAN. *(Stopping what she's doing.)* You have an audition?

Lil' Mama, you didn't tell me that.

LIL' MAMA. It's nothing, Ma.

LILLIAN. *(Hurt.)* You told daddy and you didn't tell me?

Lil' Mama/?

LIL' MAMA. Cause—

NELLY. Well, shit, what's the play?

LILLIAN. Lil' Mama, why didn't you tell me?

NELLY. I be in plays. I be in all the plays.

LILLIAN. You in plays cause I was in plays.

NELLY. I'm in plays to redeem the family name after you wreaked havoc on the school musical all them/ years.

LILLIAN. Please! Only reason they let you sing at all is because of the reputation *I established/* all them years.

NELLY. You sure did have a reputation.

> (*To* **LIL' MAMA.**)

Sang flat as a tack's head, she did.

Flat as a pancake.

Flat as an ironing board./

Flat as –

LILLIAN. You still/ going?

NELLY. Still going.

Flat as...

Shit, flat as her own ass.

LILLIAN. My ass is not flat!

If you don't stop spouting these/ LIES.

> (**NELLY** *crosses behind* **LILLIAN** *to inspect.*)

NELLY. *(Re* **LILLIAN**'s *backside.)* Where is the lie? Really, where is it?

LILLIAN. Wash those dishes.

NELLY. *(To* **LIL' MAMA.**) Mama always had me sit between them at church to help guide her tone deaf ass back to the key.

LILLIAN. *I'm* tone deaf? *Me?*

NELLY. Apparently you deaf deaf too.

> (**MAMA** *slowly makes her way down the stairs back to the kitchen.*)

LILLIAN. Where was I tone deaf? Matta fact, just bring the videos out.

NELLY. Bring 'em out then.

LILLIAN. I don't even have to prove myself cause the shit is on tape.

MAMA. That mouth, Lillian.

> *(To* **NELLY.**)

And them beans don't look blanched.

NELLY. She's still snapping!

MAMA. Are your hands broken?

NELLY. I did my half –

MAMA. *(Re dishes.)* Give me that. I'll do that. You/ help her.

LILLIAN. Mama, please remind her what the choir director used to tell you about me./

She's having a hard time remembering this morning.//

NELLY. *(To LIL' MAMA, correcting.)* You supposed to take off the ends. You can't just do it in half.

MAMA. //What Miss Nancy used to tell me about what?

LILLIAN. That I could've really/ done something with my voice.

NELLY. That you could've really done something with your voice? She told EVERYONE that.

LILLIAN. She did not!

MAMA. What are y'all fussing about now?

NELLY. Lil' Mama auditioning for a musical.

LIL' MAMA. No, she not.

NELLY. You just said/ that –

LIL' MAMA. Nope.

MAMA. Lil' Mama, you know the Tucker women are known all over ALL OVER for our voices.

NELLY. I don't think that's true.

LIL' MAMA. It's not even a/ musical.

MAMA. You're mumbling.

What's the play?

LIL' MAMA. It's okay, Imma just wait for daddy/ to get here

MAMA. Wait for daddy? That man ain't gonna be able to teach you nothing 'bout no play. You got the founder and director emeritus of the Mt. Vernon High Dramatic League as well as the first soloist at the Greater Centennial A.M.E. Zion Church lead pastor Reverend Winston Rice for the past fifteen years sitting here talking to you asking you what's the play and you gonna say "it's okay, Imma just wait for daddy." *Daddy?*

LIL' MAMA. It's not even a musical!

MAMA. *(I'll say it again.)* Founder and director emeritus of the Mt./ Vernon High Dramatic League –

LIL' MAMA. *(Giving in.)* It's Shakespeare!

NELLY. Oooo, love me a Shakespeare!

> (**NELLY** *clears her throat dramatically.*)

LILLIAN. Here we go.

NELLY. *To be, or not to be, that is the question:*

> *Whether it's better in the mind to suffer*

> *The sleighs and arrows of miserable/ fortune*

LILLIAN. Those are not the words.

NELLY. How she gonna tell me? If anyone knows the Shakespeare, it's me. I did Hamlet. I was/ Hamlet.

LILLIAN. Not the words.

NELLY. Mama, tell her them the words.

MAMA. Them not the words, baby.

Where's my purse?

LILLIAN. Why, what you need?

MAMA. My medicine.

LILLIAN. Mama…

MAMA. Don't start with me, Lillian.

LILLIAN. You said one a/ day.

MAMA. *(Ignoring **LILLIAN**.)* Which Shakespeare, Lil'?

LIL' MAMA. … Richard the III.

(A brief pause.)

NELLY. Which one is/ that again?

LILLIAN. Yeah, I don't remember that one.

MAMA. *(Announcing.)* The tragedy of Richard the III. And you're up for the role of Queen/

LIL' MAMA. Elizabeth.

MAMA. Yes. Yes yes yes.

NELLY. Wait, wait, wait, I know! Someone wants to be king?

And he'll do anything in his power to get it?

LILLIAN. That's all of 'em.

> *(The phone rings. **LILLIAN**, closest, crosses to answer.)*

NELLY. Witches?

MAMA. No, baby. Ain't no witches.

NELLY. So then how it go?

MAMA. *(Correcting.)* How does/ it go.

LILLIAN. *(Answering the phone.)* Tucker residence. Who's this?

> *(**LILLIAN** is suddenly very aware of the others in the room. She lowers her voice and goes off to a corner of the kitchen to take the call. **NELLY** makes a point to tune in on **LILLIAN**'s conversation. She's not eavesdropping per se, just actively listening.)*

LIL' MAMA. Richard wants to be king.

NELLY. I said that.

LIL' MAMA. No, you said *someone* wants to be king.

NELLY. Well, obviously I meant him.

LIL' MAMA. But that's not what you said.

LILLIAN. *(On the phone.)* Now is not a good/ time.

MAMA. You got the neck bone?

LILLIAN. *(On the phone.)* We're busy

> *(Answering* **MAMA.***)*

In the fridge.

MAMA. What good are they in the fridge, Lillian?

LILLIAN. *(To* **MAMA.***)* Well, that's where they are.

> *(Back to phone.)*

Yes, hello?

> *(**MAMA** sucks her teeth, takes out the neck bone and begins to take them out of their packaging.)*

NELLY. *(To* **LIL' MAMA.***)* Richard wants to be king and then…?

LIL' MAMA. And then kills everyone and they mamas too in order to be king.

NELLY. *(Reiterating.)* He does everything in his power.

Killing included. S'what I said.

LIL' MAMA. Not what you said.

NELLY. *(To* **MAMA.***)* Didn't I say that?

MAMA. Yes, but Richard is really about the women. That's what they won't tell you.

NELLY. How's Richard about the/ women?

MAMA. *(Noticing* **LIL' MAMA**'s *work.)* Lil' Mama, if you snapping all this off the end, what are the people gonna have left to eat?

NELLY. *(To* **LIL' MAMA.**) Told you.

LIL' MAMA. First it's too big, now it's too small. I don't know what y'all want from me!

LILLIAN. *(Still on the phone.)* Yes.

I need more time/. I –

NELLY. *(To* **LIL' MAMA.**) Your mama didn't teach you how to snap beans?

LILLIAN. *(Interjecting while still on the phone.)* She knows how to snap beans.

      (Back to the phone.)

Mmhmm.

NELLY. Apparently not.

MAMA. *(Demonstrating.)* Take one. Snip off the ends/.

You can twirl it with your finger.

Then snap it in // half. Easy.

Do it like that every time, okay?

LILLIAN. I'll call you back.

//I said I'll call you back.

I have to go.

LIL' MAMA. For all these?

MAMA. All these. And there's more in the fridge.

Nelly, blanch them in batches.

I'll be back.

LILLIAN. *(On the phone.)* I have to go.

(**MAMA** *exits.* **LILLIAN** *hangs up.*)

LIL' MAMA. Can I get another job?

LILLIAN. *(To* **NELLY.***)* Where she go?

NELLY. Where you think?

(*Re phone call.*)

What was that about?

LILLIAN. What was –? Oh, J.R.

LIL' MAMA. That was daddy?

When's he/ coming?

NELLY. What he say?

LILLIAN. *(To* **NELLY.***)* He said mind your business.

(*To* **LIL' MAMA.***)*

Let's hear it, Lil' Mama.

LIL' MAMA. Hear what?

LILLIAN. This audition. You gotta practice, don't you?

I can help.

LIL' MAMA. I don't want to.

LILLIAN. Lil' Mama...

LIL' MAMA. I don't know it by heart yet!

LILLIAN. You don't have to know it by heart.

NELLY. Go get the words. I'll help you.

LILLIAN. If anyone will be helping her, it will be me.

NELLY. Let her tell it you the last one she wanna be practicing with.

LILLIAN. Shut up, Nelly.

(To **LIL' MAMA.***)*

Go get your words. Quickly.

*(***LIL' MAMA*** exits up the stairs.)*

NELLY. Rather spend time with daddy. Don't got no use for
mommy.

LILLIAN. Shut up.

NELLY. I'm just going off what the little girl/ said.

LILLIAN. I said shut up.

NELLY. I heard what you said. I'm still talking. Gonna keep
talking. Talking,/ talking, talking.

LILLIAN. Whatever.

You're a child.

> *(***NELLY*** takes the snapped string beans,
> transfers them to a sieve, and brings them to
> the stove to blanch, teasing* **LILLIAN** *the entire
> way.)*

NELLY. Apparently daddy don't wanna spend no time with
mommy either?

LILLIAN. Excuse me?

NELLY. I heard you and Mama talking.

Y'all been "having a hard time"?

LILLIAN. She told you that?

NELLY. And money's tight?

LILLIAN. Did Mama tell you that?

NELLY. Might've slipped.

LILLIAN. ... Well, that's not what I said.

NELLY. It was something like that.

LILLIAN. We're fine.

NELLY. Come on, I won't tell.

(Maybe **LILLIAN** *contemplates confiding in* **NELLY** *for a moment.)*

LILLIAN. ... You wouldn't understand.

Grown folks business.

NELLY. I'm grown.

LILLIAN. Nelly, you so far from grown you can't even see the edge of it. Trust me.

NELLY. Well, what makes you grown then?

I look after the house, help with the bills.

LILLIAN. Give it time.

NELLY. I've been taking care of Mama. That's more than you can say.

LILLIAN. Mama takes care of you.

NELLY. You don't know what happens in this house, Lillian. You left.

LILLIAN. For Christ sakes, yes. I left. People leave.

NELLY. And as soon as I turn eighteen, that's just what Imma do.

Already got it planned out. Been saving money for months.

LILLIAN. Oh yeah? And where are you planning to go?

NELLY. Far away as I can.

... California.

Gonna drive the whole way.

See the country.

I'm trying out for all the big ones. USC. UCLA.

Long as it's out there I don't care which one it is.

LILLIAN. She'll never let you go.

NELLY. Well, she can't keep me here.

LILLIAN. Why are you so pressed to be gone?

NELLY. Why are you so pressed to be back?

LILLIAN. That boy?

NELLY. *(A correction.)* My man and I are gonna build a life together.

He's just waiting on me to graduate.

LILLIAN. Y'all gonna build a house together too?

NELLY. Maybe we will.

LILLIAN. You sound stupid.

NELLY. You sound jealous.

LILLIAN. Okay,/ Nelly.

NELLY. You're jealous cause your life now is what it's gonna be and mine is just starting.

LILLIAN. I said okay.

NELLY. You think I want what you want?

LILLIAN. I think you don't know what you want.

NELLY. I know exactly what I want.

LILLIAN. Give it time.

NELLY. For what? Time don't make you nothing but old, sick and dead.

Everything I want is right now.

I got a man that wants me right now and he wants me often.

In the street, in the store. Don't matter where we are.

He be up my shirt pulling me into him with one hand and the other hand he got grabbing my ass, and he be kissing me like he's trying to – I don't know – scoop my soul out with his tongue. Like he don't want there to be none of me left.

And hell, I don't even care if there's any left of me or not.

LILLIAN. ... That's fucking nasty.

NELLY. No, it ain't nasty. It's natural.

LILLIAN. Won't last. All that "natural".

NELLY. Why? Why my life gotta end up like you and her? Why do you want that for me? I'm telling you I'm in love you telling me I'm stupid!

> (**NELLY** *heads to the stove to remove the string beans and dump the water.*)

LILLIAN. That's not – Okay, Nelly. Fine.

NELLY. It *is* fine.

LILLIAN. That's what I said.

NELLY. That's all you ever say –

> (*Out of the blue,* **NELLY** *loses her balance. She stumbles a little, catching herself just in time to prevent the hot water from spilling everywhere. Some of the water splashes on the floor. It's scary for a second.*)

LILLIAN. What happened?!

NELLY. It's nothing.

LILLIAN. What do you mean nothing? You almost dropped the whole pot!

NELLY. I said it's nothing!

LILLIAN. Well, sit down, shit.

> (*She helps* **NELLY** *to a chair.*)

What was that?

NELLY. I get dizzy sometimes.

LILLIAN. You get dizzy?

NELLY. Yeah.

LILLIAN. How often is sometimes?

NELLY. Comes and goes.

LILLIAN. Comes and goes?

NELLY. That's what I said.

LILLIAN. What comes and goes?

Nelly?

> (**NELLY** *looks at* **LILLIAN** *before dropping her eyes.* **LILLIAN** *understands. Quiet.*)

Nelly...

NELLY. I said it's nothing. Get out my face.

> (**NELLY** *gets up to return to her work.* **LILLIAN** *reaches for her, catching just the back of her shirt, which tightens around* **NELLY***'s stomach as she does.* **NELLY** *instinctively brings her hands to her stomach in attempt to cover herself.* **LILLIAN** *backs away.*)

LILLIAN. What are you [covering]...?

> (**NELLY** *looks at* **LILLIAN** *before dropping her eyes.* **LILLIAN** *understands. Quiet.*)

How far?

NELLY. Known a few weeks.

LILLIAN. A few weeks?

NELLY. ...

LILLIAN. Did you tell her?

NELLY. No, I didn't tell her.

LILLIAN. So who knows about this?

NELLY. ... You.

LILLIAN. You've been to a doctor?/ Who's is it?

NELLY. Yes, I been to the – It's his!

LILLIAN. You sure?

NELLY. Yes, I'm sure. Jesus, Lillian.

> (**NELLY** *shakes* **LILLIAN** *off and returns to the spill.* **LILLIAN** *keeps her eyes on* **NELLY**, *incredulous.*)

LILLIAN. My god.

NELLY. Don't get all hot and bothered.

LILLIAN. You're seventeen.

NELLY. *You* were seventeen.

... And I'm not keeping it.

LILLIAN. Excuse me?

NELLY. I'm not/ keeping –

LILLIAN. Oh my god.

If she found out you were even thinking [about] – and today of all/ days –

NELLY. *(A threat.)* She won't though.

> *(Beat.)*

LILLIAN. *(A new approach.)* Look, I know this is scary, and you probably have a million things running around in your head, but you can't just – you have to THINK these things/ through –

NELLY. I have thought about it! You think I haven't thought about it? You think I'm not thinking about it every/ second.

LILLIAN. God, can you just – listen! Can you just imagine not knowing for one second? Trust/ me.

NELLY. Trust you?

LILLIAN. These things – you have to be... You have to be sure about them. You don't get to take them back.

NELLY. Were you sure?

LILLIAN. *(Taken aback.)* I love my children. I love my children more than anything.

NELLY. *(She needs this.)* Yeah, but were you sure? Tell me the truth.

Were you sure?

LILLIAN. ... Yes. Yes.

> *(Pause.)*

I mean... of course, there are days when you – God... ummm – Yes, there are days when you wonder, you know, what if, uh, something different? Not every day, but – there are days.

> *(Pause.)*

NELLY. Well, I don't want it.

I don't want a single one of those/ days

I know what I know now.

I know what I know now and what I know now is that I can't –

and I – I only told you cause// I thought...

cause I'm...

LILLIAN. Nelly.

//Nelly...

NELLY. Just leave me alone about it!

I don't know why I told you.

>*(Silence. Kitchen business resumes.)*

LILLIAN. You have to tell her.

NELLY. You don't get to tell me what to do.

>*(**LILLIAN** stops her busywork and looks directly at **NELLY**.)*

LILLIAN. You tell her or I will.

>*(They hold each other's gaze for a moment. **LILLIAN** returns to her work.)*

Scene Three

(Later in the Tucker Kitchen.)

(LIL' MAMA at the stove standing over the big pot. A spoon sits idle in the stew, but she isn't stirring. Instead, she reads from a few loose pieces of paper. She is practicing for her audition, using the opportunity of the empty kitchen to really give it her all.)

LIL' MAMA. *ah my poor princes*

ah my tender babes my... unborn –?

flowers! new-appealing sweets,

if yet your... souls souls GENTLE souls fly in the... sky?

(She cheats, looking quickly at the papers.)

Air! Gentle souls fly in the air –

(MAMA enters.)

MAMA. Why are you in here by yourself?

LIL' MAMA. *(Still focused on her papers.)* I don't know.

MAMA. Well, where is everyone?

LIL' MAMA. I don't know.

MAMA. Did someone at least start the dumplings?

LIL' MAMA. I don't know.

MAMA. *(Re the stew.)* Lil Mama, why you got this all the way on high? This is my good pot!

LIL' MAMA. I don't know!

MAMA. Well move!

LIL' MAMA. She just said stir!

MAMA. Go under there and get me another pot! This is my good pot!

> (**LIL' MAMA** *goes under the sink and pulls out a sauce pan, offers it to* **MAMA**.)

What am I supposed to do with that itty-bitty pot? Get me a big pot like this one!

LIL' MAMA. You didn't specify!

> (**LIL' MAMA** *pulls out a big pot and hands it to* **MAMA** *who immediately starts transferring the contents of the first pot.*)

MAMA. Get the ladle over there and scrape these beans off the bottom. I don't know what anyone is thinking leaving the kitchen with all this stuff cooking –

> (*The phone rings.*)

And who keeps calling my house this early!

> (*To* **LIL' MAMA**, *re the pot.*)

Come do this!

> (**LIL' MAMA** *crosses to take over the pot scraping as* **MAMA** *goes to answer the phone.*)

(*On the phone, skrong-like.*) Hello?
Hello?

> (*She hangs up.*)

Harassing me on a Saturday morning.

> (*To* **LIL' MAMA**.)

You got all the beans off the bottom? I just want the beans, I don't want none of the other stuff.

(*Everything is frustrating her now.*)

What are these papers doing in the kitchen? What are these papers?

(**LIL' MAMA** *quickly goes to scoop up the papers, but* **MAMA** *beats her to it.*)

LIL' MAMA. It's nothing...

I was practicing.

MAMA. (*Softening.*) These your lines?

LIL' MAMA. Yeah...

MAMA. The Richard?

LIL' MAMA. Yeah...

MAMA. Richard, Richard, Richard.

(**MAMA** *looks over the papers, taking in the text.*)

LIL' MAMA. It's okay. I'll take 'em upstairs.

MAMA. No, go on. I'll read with you.

LIL' MAMA. Right now?

MAMA. Yes, right now.

LIL' MAMA. I'm not really ready –

MAMA. Wrong answer. What if I was a director walked right in here right now, and I said, "Lil' Mama, I wanna hear your Elizabeth, we going to Broadway tomorrow" you gonna say/ "I'm not really ready?"

LIL' MAMA. I don't think a director would walk right in *here* and say –

(*Off of* **MAMA**'s *look.*)

No, I wouldn't say that, I guess.

MAMA. Alright. So. Elizabeth. Action.

LIL' MAMA. It's not all the way memorized and you would have to read/ the –

MAMA. Little. Mama.

LIL' MAMA. Alright, alright! I'll do it.

> (**LIL' MAMA** *comes out from behind the island,
> clears her throat, checks back in with* **MAMA,**
> *and takes a moment to center herself. Then:)*

Ah, my poor princes! Ah, my tender babes,

My unblown flowers, new-appealing/ sweets

MAMA. appearing

LIL' MAMA. Huh?

MAMA. It's "new-*appearing* sweets"

LIL' MAMA. Really? Let me see.

MAMA. Lil' Mama, I'm looking right at the page.

LIL' MAMA. *(With attitude.) new appearing sweets.*

If yet your souls—GENTLE souls fly in the... air?

And be not fixed in doom perpetual

Hover about me with your airy wings

And hear your mother's lament/ation.

MAMA. What do you mean by mother's lamentation?

LIL' MAMA. Huh?

MAMA. What do you mean by mother's lamentation?

LIL' MAMA. Well, she/

MAMA. *(A correction.) I*

LIL' MAMA. What?

MAMA. She is you. You is she.

"What *I* mean by mother's lamentation is" …

LIL' MAMA. *(Really not feeling this.)* I really don't wanna—can I just do the words?

MAMA. Yeah, you can just do the words and just not get the part/ –

LIL' MAMA. *(Relenting.)* My son died!

MAMA. Yes. Your son—your son he… Well, did he just up and die?

LIL' MAMA. *(Deep sigh.)* No. He was murdered.

MAMA. MURDERED! And there was nothing to be done. There was – was there anything to be done?

LIL' MAMA. I suppose she could've –

MAMA. *I! I* could've!

LIL' MAMA. *I* could've tried to stop/ it –

MAMA. You didn't know! You didn't know.

And you did. You did try to stop it. Didn't you?

LIL' MAMA. Yeah, but maybe not hard enough? I didn't try hard enough.

MAMA. *(Pained.)* Oh.

Oh.

And…?

LIL' MAMA. *(Stumped.)* And…?

MAMA. And this makes you feel…?

LIL' MAMA. …

MAMA. This is a mother who is mourning the death of her son.

Her son.

Her boy.

Her baby.

This is a devastation unlike [ ]

And this makes you feel...?

LIL' MAMA. Sad!

MAMA. Sad?

LIL' MAMA. I mean, I guess.

MAMA. You guess?

LIL' MAMA. I don't know!

MAMA. You gotta put some uumph in it.

LIL' MAMA. Uumph?

MAMA. Yes, uumph. They not teaching you about uumph at the school?

LIL' MAMA. No, they not teaching us about uumph at the school.

> (**MAMA** *reaches into a pack of sweet potatoes and hands her one.*)

MAMA. Here.

LIL' MAMA. What's this?

MAMA. That's your baby.

LIL' MAMA. My/ what?

MAMA. Do it again, but talk to your baby.

LIL' MAMA. That's a sweet potato.

MAMA. And are you an actor or not? Now, take it from the top.

> (**LIL' MAMA** *is not feeling this.*)

LIL' MAMA. *Ah, my poor princes,/ ah my tender babes.*

My unblown flowers,// new-appearing sweets,

if yet your gentle souls fly in the air///

and be not fixed in doom perpetual

MAMA. Look at your son.

//Remember, that's your dead baby in your arms.

/// You can't just say the words, Lil' Mama. You have to hold them. And in your bones, you have to hold them.

LIL' MAMA. *If yet your gentle souls fly in the air*

And be not fixed in doom perpetual

Hover about me with your airy wings

And hear your mother's...

hear your mother's...

And hear your... your... ugh, what's the word?

MAMA. *(Hand over her heart.)* You forgetting the words because you don't know it here.

LIL' MAMA. I'm forgetting the words cause I don't have it memorized!

MAMA. *(Re the sweet potato.)* Give it here.

LIL' MAMA. What?

MAMA. Give the baby here. You gotta earn the baby.

LIL' MAMA. It's a stupid sweet potato!

> *(**LIL' MAMA** tosses the sweet potato on the counter. **NELLY** comes down the stairs heading straight for the back door.)*

MAMA. *(To **NELLY**.)* Where do you think you're going?

NELLY. To the corner store. I'm thirsty.

> *(**MAMA** turns on the kitchen sink faucet.)*

MAMA. Glasses in the cupboard.

NELLY. Damn, Mama.

MAMA. Cuss one more time in my house.

One. More./ Time.

NELLY. Fine.

MAMA. You know y'all burnt my pot? My good pot? I go upstairs for one second, everyone has something better to do.

> *(The phone rings.* **NELLY,** *closest, goes to answer.)*

(To **NELLY,** *re the caller.)* Tell 'em if I didn't have it last week and I didn't have it yesterday what makes them think I have it today.

NELLY. *(Pausing before answering.)* I'm not gonna tell – Can you tell them that?

MAMA. *(Through her teeth.)* Answer the phone.

> *(To herself.)*

I don't know what they want from me.

NELLY. Tucker residence?

Who's/ this?

MAMA. Can't even lie down for a minute.

Lil' Mama, get me a bowl for the dumplings.

> *(***LIL' MAMA*** does.)*

NELLY. Yes, Tucker residence.

No, this is Nelly.

MAMA. *(To* **NELLY.***)* Who is it?

NELLY. Hello?

Hello?

> (**NELLY** *hangs up.*)

MAMA. Who was it?

NELLY. Someone calling for Lillian.

MAMA. J.R.?

NELLY. Didn't sound like J.R.

MAMA. Hmm.

Did you take out the tomatoes?

NELLY. Lil' Mama, did you take out the tomatoes?

LIL' MAMA. You didn't tell me to do that.

NELLY. Yes, I did!

> (**NELLY** *rushes to the oven.* **LILLIAN** *comes down the stairs.*)

MAMA. They better not be burnt too, Nelly.

NELLY. It's fine, it's fine.

MAMA. No, it is not fine. It is – the opposite of fine!

LILLIAN. Lil' Mama, you took the tomatoes out the oven? Mama, why aren't you lying/ down?

MAMA. *(To anyone who will listen now.)* My pot is burnt.

LILLIAN. What?

NELLY. I got the tomatoes! They're fine.

MAMA. My pot is burnt.

My *good* pot.

LILLIAN. *(To* **LIL' MAMA.***)* Lil' Mama, I told you to keep stirring!/ I'm sorry, Mama.

LIL' MAMA. I did!

MAMA. Oh, she did. But you had the doggone thing up on high and all the beans stuck to the bottom. We already had to start over once. I can not afford to do it again a third time.

(LILLIAN *crosses to look in the pot.*)

LILLIAN. It'll be fine.

MAMA. How you gonna tell me how it's gonna be like I haven't been making the stew. Like I don't know how to make the stew. *It'll be fine.* That's why I just do everything by myself, cause I can't trust no one to do it for me. I go lie down for one second./ One second!

LILLIAN. Alright, Mama.

(MAMA'*s hot and bothered now, so she's just going to keep talking. She moves through the kitchen with no real goal. Picking things up, putting things back down somewhere different. The following rant is full of gesticulative magic. She is acting it out, okay? Making us see it. The others watch her work herself up and, after a while, all take a stab at impersonating her behind her back. Somewhere in the middle of this, the four of them are synchronized. They know each other's bodies so well.)*

MAMA. and, then, of course, while I'm up there that damn dog won't stop yelping. You know, I just want to rest my eyes for half a second and yelp yelp yelp yelp yelp.

So I look out my window and of course it's Beverly's raggedy self leaning up on my fence smoking her refer. Evil ol' dog tied to the pole making a mess everywhere. You know, I don't usually say nothing bout no one, but she just gets me going, she really do. And, of course, she don't have no baggies with her, nothing. So I say, uh, Beverly, you gonna clean that up when he's done, right?

And she just gonna go "humph". What's that? *Humph.*
And it ain't no regular "humph"; she say it with her
neck and shoulders. All this *(She demonstrates.)* How
she gonna get an attitude with me – *with me!* – and
she the one degrading the neighborhood with the dog
mess? But, of course, she don't have no home training
cause look at her kids. Almost had to check her, almost
did, but I'm saved and she better be glad for it cause she
got me upset with that, she really did. So then I come
down here, try to cool off in the kitchen since I can't
rest in my own bedroom, and not a soul in sight. Lil'
Mama in here don't know what she doing, don't have
no clear direction, stew splashing and spilling all over
the floor – I guess everyone wanna eat the stew, but
don't nobody wanna make the stew. I mean I step out
the room for wasn't even a millisecond, I come back,
everyone found something better to do, the phone is
ringing off the hook, the house nearly burning down
and I can't afford it!

LILLIAN. Phone rang?

MAMA. Yes. The phone rang.

NELLY. Again.

LILLIAN. Who was it?

NELLY. Some man asking for you.

LILLIAN. Asking for me? You mean J.R.?

NELLY. No, I don't mean J.R. I mean some man asked for
you and then hung up.

LILLIAN. Oh. That's weird.

NELLY. Yeah, it is weird. Who was it?

LILLIAN. How I'm supposed to know? Probably wrong
number.

NELLY. How it's the wrong number if they asking for you?

LILLIAN. Sometimes they get your name from a list or something.

There have been a lot of strange men calling the house lately.

(A threat.)

Wouldn't you agree?

NELLY. *(Tense.)* I would.

MAMA. Well, maybe it's time to change my number then. The way Wells Fargo calls here. Nelly, get the flour down and start the dough.

(The phone rings. Moment of truth. LILLIAN *and* NELLY *both look to* MAMA, *exchange a brief glance and beeline for it.)*

NELLY. I got it!

MAMA. Nelly, didn't I just/ say

LILLIAN. It's fine, I can get it.

*(*NELLY *grabs the phone first, but* LILLIAN *wrestles it out of her hand.)*

NELLY. What is wrong with you!

LILLIAN. Give me the phone, Nelly!

NELLY. I got to it first!

MAMA. What are y'all –

Would y'all stop!

Acting like children.

*(*NELLY *succeeds.)*

NELLY. *(Into the receiver.)* Hello?

MAMA. Who is it?

NELLY. *(Realizing who it is.)* Junior?

Where are you?

MAMA. That's Junior?

LILLIAN. Give me the phone.

NELLY. Yes, we're all here.

> *(LILLIAN snatches the phone from NELLY. Throughout, the passing of the phone, which happens swiftly and seamlessly, takes place above MAMA's head. MAMA misses her turn each time by an inch.)*

LILLIAN. *(Into the receiver.)* Junior? Boy, where are you?

MAMA. Let me/ speak to him!

LILLIAN. *(Into the receiver.)* Yes, we're all here.

Waiting on you.

You need to come on now.

> *(LILLIAN holds out the phone to LIL' MAMA.)*

MAMA. Let me speak/ to him –

LIL' MAMA. *(Into the receiver.)* Where are you?

Yes, we're all here waiting on you.

You need to come on now.

It's time.

> *(LIL' MAMA hangs up.)*

MAMA. I said I wanted to speak/ to him!

LILLIAN. He'll be here soon.

> *(Picking up LIL' MAMA's papers off the counter.)*

What are these papers?

LIL' MAMA. It's nothing.

LILLIAN. Lil' Mama, these your words?

LIL' MAMA. I'm not doing it no more.

MAMA. She knows the words just fine. She was just doing it for me.

Nelly, the dough.

LIL' MAMA. I'm not even gonna go.

LILLIAN. Why not?

MAMA. She got an attitude 'cause she hasn't earned her baby.

NELLY. Earned her/ what?

LILLIAN. Her baby?

LIL' MAMA. *(With much attitude.)* I don't have an attitude.

LILLIAN. I'll do it with you, Lil' Mama. I'll be the duchess.

MAMA. Excuse me. The play is already cast.

LILLIAN. Lil' Mama, who would you rather read with you?

MAMA. You snooze, you lose, Lillian.

NELLY. *(Reaching for the sides.)* Well how many parts is it?

MAMA. Lil Mama, if you'd rather have these amateurs –

LILLIAN. Amateurs?

NELLY. Mama, you tryna start something?

MAMA. AMATEURS over me who, might I remind you, was the founder and director emeritus of the

MAMA/LILLIAN/ NELLY. *(Though* **MAMA** *trails off as she realizes she's being mocked.)* Mt. Vernon High Dramatic League and lead soloist/ at the Greater Centennial A.M.E.

MAMA. *(Ignoring them.)* WHO taught both of them everything they know about the dramatic arts –

NELLY. The *dramatic arts*?

LILLIAN. Just let her practice the words. Please.

MAMA. Fine.

LIL' MAMA. I don't have it memorized.

LILLIAN. Even a little?

LIL' MAMA. *(Indicating her heart.)* She says I have to know it here.

LILLIAN. Just do what you do know.

Go head.

> *(**LIL' MAMA** looks at her kinfolk. This is just the situation she was trying to avoid. She sighs heavily. Crosses in front of the counter. Prepares to start.)*

LIL' MAMA. *Ah/—*

LILLIAN. Probably wanna take a deep breath before you start, Lil'.

> *(**LIL' MAMA** glares at **LILLIAN**. Takes the deep breath.)*

LIL' MAMA. *Ah,/ my—*

NELLY. Well, don't lean to the side like that. Gotta, you know, be grounded.

LILLIAN. Unless you want to and that's a choice.

> *(**LIL' MAMA** looks at **NELLY**. Adjusts her stance.)*

LIL' MAMA. *Ah, my/ poor—*

LILLIAN. But don't look at the ground.

NELLY. You can look at the ground.

LILLIAN. It makes her look unsure.

NELLY. Well, maybe her character is unsure.

LILLIAN. *(To* **LIL' MAMA.***)* You want to see your audience, Lil' Mama. Try it, see how you feel.

NELLY. I disagree.

LILLIAN. *(Ignoring* **NELLY.***)* Go ahead.

> *(***LIL' MAMA** *is mortified.)*

LIL' MAMA. *Ah, my poor/ princes, ah*HHHHHHHH
HHHHHHH

I'M NOT DOING IT!

LILLIAN. Remember your deep breath!

> *(Responding to* **LIL' MAMA***'s outburst.)*

What's wrong? You're doing great!

MAMA. Doing great doing what? You didn't let her get two words out!

LILLIAN. She's nervous.

LIL' MAMA. I'm not/ nervous!

MAMA. She's not nervous.

NELLY. Lil' Mama, you just gotta dress it up, show us something.

LIL' MAMA. Show you what?

LILLIAN. All you gotta do is put a little bit of feeling in it.

LIL' MAMA. I was feeling!

NELLY. *(Snatching the paper.)* Lil' Mama, you gotta do it like this.

> *(Finding her place on the page.)*

So many miseries have crazed my voice

That my woe-wearied tongue is still and/ mute

LILLIAN. Uh uh! I'm the duchess!

NELLY. You snooze, you lose, Lillian.

Let me get the baby.

MAMA. No, you have to *earn* the baby.

LILLIAN. *(Snatching the paper.)* Watch and learn.

Dead life, blind sight, poor mortal living ghost,

Woe's scene, world's shame, grave's due by life/ usurped

MAMA. No no no no! No passion, no nothing.

NELLY. *(Teasing* **LILLIAN.***)* No passion, no nothing!

LILLIAN. Shut up!

MAMA. *(Coaching.)* Think about this woman holding her dead sons in her arms, on her knees, cursing the man who did it!

LILLIAN. Give me the baby. Imma do it again.

> *(***NELLY** *snatches a can of broth off of the counter.)*

NELLY. This my baby. Watch.

O, whoth any cause to mourn but/ we?

> *(***LILLIAN** *grabs some kitchen appliance: her own baby. She and* **NELLY** *read over one another, struggling to snatch the papers away from each other. This shouldn't be in unison. There's some kind of orchestration to this competition the players will have to find themselves. Whatever it is, it is certainly fierce. And loud.)*

LILLIAN. *If ancient sorrow be most reverend,*

NELLY. *Give mine the benefit of seigniory/,*

LILLIAN. That's not even how you say that word!

NELLY. *And let my griefs frown on the upper hand.*

LILLIAN. *If sorrow can admit society/,*

NELLY. *Tell o'er your woes again by/ viewing mine.*

NELLY. Get off of me!

> *(Several of the papers fall to the floor and the show unravels. Do they all of a sudden somehow know these words by heart? It is no longer fun. It is mean.)*

LILLIAN/ NELLY. (**LILLIAN** *joining in again.*) *I had an Edward till a Richard killed him;*

> *I had a husband till/ a Richard killed him.*

NELLY. You doing too much!

LILLIAN. All you doing is being loud about it. Screaming about it don't make it good.

NELLY. I'm not screaming, I'm projecting. PROJECTING.

> *(**NELLY** gets in **LILLIAN**'s face.)*

LILLIAN. You better get out my face, Nelly.

NELLY. Or what. Orwhatorwhatorwhatorwhatorwhat.

LILLIAN. You better get out my face/NELLY.

NELLY. Ain't nobody scared of you!

> *(In the midst of all this, **MAMA** grabs hold of an idle sweet potato on the kitchen counter and starts up a simple, chilling:)*

MAMA. *If ancient sorrow be most reverend,*

> *Give mine the benefit of seigniory,*

> *And let my griefs frown on the upper hand.*

If sorrow can admit society,

Tell o'er your woes again by viewing mine.

I had an Edward till a Richard killed him;

I had a husband till a Richard killed him;

Thou hadst an Edward till a Richard killed him;

Thou hadst a Richard till a Richard killed him.

> *(Everything hangs midair. Then* **MAMA** *exhales and the room falls back into place. She can do that. Make us forget where we are standing. Make us long for something we didn't know we were missing. Hell, she wasn't the founder and director emeritus of the Mt. Vernon High Dramatic League as well as the lead soprano at the Greater Centennial A.M.E. Zion Church lead by Pastor Winston Rice for the past fifteen years for no reason. The rest of the women watch her in awe.)*

Scene Four

(The Tucker kitchen. Several hours later.)

(The kitchen is empty. Everything on the stove is cooking down on its own. The phone rings. No one answers. The ringing picks up again for another round. No one answers. Just as the ringing begins again, **NELLY** *enters to answer it. The ringing stops just before she makes it to the phone. After a moment of consideration (and checking to make sure no one is around), she picks it up anyway.)*

(She listens.)

(She listens.)

(Her eyes widen.)

(She covers her mouth.)

(She listens.)

(...)

(The call ends. She stands there stunned for a moment with the phone hanging in her hand. Processing. So much so that she doesn't notice **LIL' MAMA** *enter laden with several aluminum trays, bunsen burners, potatoes, etc. from the pantry. All far too heavy for her little arms to carry.)*

LIL' MAMA. Umm, hello.

NELLY. Huh?

LIL' MAMA. Can you help?

> (**NELLY** *snaps back into it, crossing to help* **LIL'
> MAMA** *get the bags onto the counter.*)

NELLY. What's all this stuff?

LIL' MAMA. She said we wasn't gonna have enough.

NELLY. This is from the pantry?

LIL' MAMA. I guess.

NELLY. Where is she?

LIL' MAMA. I don't/ know.

> (**LILLIAN** *comes down the stairs, a little on
> edge.*)

LILLIAN. What's all this stuff?

NELLY. She said we wasn't gonna have enough.

> (**LILLIAN** *rummages through the stuff on the
> counter.*)

LILLIAN. *(To* **LIL' MAMA.***)* This is for the stew?

NELLY. I don't/ know.

LILLIAN. This isn't all gonna get done in time.

NELLY. Always does.

LILLIAN. *(To* **LIL' MAMA.***)* Put this away.

> *(To* **NELLY.***)*

You check the oven?

NELLY. I'm not the oven checker.

> (**LILLIAN,** *sucking her teeth, crosses to check
> the oven.*)

LIL' MAMA. *(To* **MAMA.***)* Where do I put this?

LILLIAN. *(Snappy.)* I don't know where that goes.

LIL' MAMA. I'm just asking.

NELLY. *(To* **LILLIAN.***)* Why you all stressed out?

LILLIAN. Who says I'm stressed out?

LIL' MAMA. *(Re another item.)* What about this?

LILLIAN. *(Snappy still.)* I said I don't know, Lil' Mama!

NELLY. Seem like you stressed out.

LIL' MAMA. Is daddy almost here?

LILLIAN. Daddy will be here.

NELLY. When?

> *(***LIL' MAMA** *climbs up onto a chair to reach the cabinets on top of the fridge.)*

LILLIAN. He'll –

> *(Seeing* **LIL' MAMA.***)*

Lil' Mama, have you lost your mind!

LIL' MAMA. You said you didn't know!

LILLIAN. GET down.

LIL' MAMA. What'd I do?

NELLY. Yeah, what'd she do?

LILLIAN. Go upstairs and get the clothes out of the dryer.

We have to start getting ourselves together now.

> *(***LIL' MAMA** *exits upstairs.* **LILLIAN** *returns to some unfinished activity on the counter. Throughout,* **NELLY** *watches* **LILLIAN** *silently, obviously waiting for some kind of engagement.)*

LILLIAN. Yes, Nelly?

NELLY. I don't got nothing to say to you.

LILLIAN. Stop looking at me then.

NELLY. Why, is there something you're hiding?

LILLIAN. You're one to talk.

NELLY. I'm not hiding.

LILLIAN. No? Then when Mama walks in here, go on lift your shirt up and let her see.

> *(Both on edge. **NELLY** adjusts her volume, very aware of the points of egress where **MAMA** might walk in at any moment. **LILLIAN** matches.)*

NELLY. I told you to mind your business.

LILLIAN. It is my business.

Mama already has enough going on.

She doesn't need any more added stress.

NELLY. Exactly. She doesn't need any more added stress. So shut up about it.

LILLIAN. As long as you're living in her house, it's gonna be her rules. If you don't like it, leave it. I left.

NELLY. And now you're back.

LILLIAN. Yes, I am back.

NELLY. Why?

LILLIAN. Why...?

NELLY. are you back? Why are you back?

> *(Maybe this catches **LILLIAN** a little off guard.)*

LILLIAN. Mama needs help.

NELLY. Mama has help.

LILLIAN. Oh yeah? Mama has help barely in the house laying on her back half the time?

NELLY. Better than help never comes around and only checks in when she needs money.

LILLIAN. Whatever, Nelly.

NELLY. Answer the question.

LILLIAN. I told you why I'm here.

NELLY. No, you told Mama why you here. I don't buy that shit for a second.

LILLIAN. She needs me/ here.

NELLY. She's been needing you here for years. She's been needing you ever since/ [ ]

LILLIAN. I don't have to explain myself to you.

NELLY. Yes, you do.

LILLIAN. No, I don't.

NELLY. Yes, you do.

LILLIAN. No, I – I'm not doing this with you.

NELLY. Seem like you hiding something

LILLIAN. I already told you/ I

NELLY. And doing a bad job about/ it, too.

LILLIAN. *(Fed up.)* I wanted to come home! I get to come home when I want! Shit!

> *(She cuts herself.)*

Dammit!

NELLY. *(Knowing.)* Yeah, well.

I don't believe you.

(LILLIAN *watches* NELLY *as she crosses back to the stove.* LIL' MAMA *reenters. She looks between the two women in the kitchen. Senses something off.*)

LIL' MAMA. *(To* MAMA.*)* You cut yourself.

LILLIAN. Yes, I cut myself.

LIL' MAMA. *(Re chopping.)* You want me to do it?

LILLIAN. I want you to finish putting up that stuff.

(MAMA *enters.*)

MAMA. Lil' Mama, leave that out. I'm just about to start that.

Y'all checked the oven?

LILLIAN. I got my eye on it.

So what's all this, Mama?

MAMA. Thought I could whip up a little potato salad or something quick. Have something on the side.

LILLIAN. We have the string beans on the side.

MAMA. Well, it'll be on the side of the side.

LILLIAN. We gotta get going, Mama.

At least make/ the first trip over.

MAMA. It'll be quick. It's/ fine.

LILLIAN. We'll pick up something extra on the way.

MAMA. There's enough extra in the house.

LILLIAN. I'll pay for it.

MAMA. Oh, Lillian, please.

LILLIAN. I said I'll pay/ for it.

MAMA. And I said it's fine.

You don't need to spend any of your money.

It's fine.

> *(Noticing everyone.)*

Why aren't y'all dressed?

NELLY. Lillian's been busy on the phone.

MAMA. Someone called?

LILLIAN. No.

NELLY. No?

MAMA. Who called? For me?

LIL' MAMA. *(Waving a bag of cornmeal.)* Where does this go?

MAMA. Leave all that out, baby. I'm gonna get to that in a second.

> *(Back to NELLY.)*

Was it someone for me?

LILLIAN. No one called.

NELLY. No? I heard the phone ring several times.

MAMA. And y'all ain't answer?

NELLY. I didn't answer.

MAMA. Probably just as good.

> *(To LIL' MAMA.)*

Bring me that Tupperware from under there. The big/
one.

NELLY. But, Lillian/...?

LILLIAN. *(A decision.)* It was J.R.

He's not coming.

(Everything stops.)

MAMA. He's not coming?

LIL' MAMA. Daddy's not coming?

NELLY. He's not coming, Lillian?

LILLIAN. Nelly.

MAMA. I thought you said –

LILLIAN. I know what I said, Mama. I tried/, but he's…

MAMA. Well, why isn't he coming?

LILLIAN. He/ just –

MAMA. *(Getting a little worked up.)* I don't even know why I try because I'm always disappointed. Always disappointed.

LILLIAN. Please don't get upset, Mama.

MAMA. How is it gonna look I been planning this thing and/ cooking all this food and I can't even get my own –

LILLIAN. Who cares what it's gonna look like?

MAMA. I care!

I don't even know why I bother.

LILLIAN. *(Fumbling.)* Mama, he's just… not up for the trip.

We'll all come another time.

MAMA. Don't lie to me on top of it, Lillian.

LILLIAN. I'm not [lying]—You know what? We'll be out of your way by tomorrow.

MAMA. Out of my way? You weren't in my/ way –

LILLIAN. Well, it seems like everything I been doing since I been here been the wrong thing!

MAMA. Who are you raising your voice at?

LILLIAN. Mama, please don't talk to me like I'm a child.

MAMA. I'm not talking to you no kind of way. I'm just talking!

NELLY. *(Teasing* **LILLIAN.***)* Talking, talking, talking.

MAMA. *(To* **NELLY.***)* Stop that!

    (Back to **LILLIAN.***)*

When were you planning to tell me this?

LILLIAN. Tell you what, Mama?

MAMA. That you were leaving, Lillian!

LILLIAN. I just found out!

MAMA. When?

LILLIAN. Just now, Mama, shit!

MAMA. Don't cuss in this house, Lillian/. I don't care how old you are.

LILLIAN. FINE. Fine.

MAMA. Why are you getting an attitude?

LIL' MAMA. Mama, we're leaving?

LILLIAN. Yes. Go upstairs and get yourself together. And call Junior.

MAMA. I'm just asking you a question!

LILLIAN. No, you're asking me the same question a hundred times! I already told you he said/ –

NELLY. What did he say, Lillian?

LILLIAN. *(To* **NELLY.***)* I swear if you don't get out/ my face...

MAMA. Why are you talking to her like that? What is wrong with you?

LIL' MAMA. Mama?

LILLIAN. Lil' Mama, how many times do I have to tell you to go upstairs?

MAMA. Hello? Are you going to answer my question?

LILLIAN. *(Snapping.)* Which one, Mama?! Shit! I can't breathe with you down my/ neck over every little—

MAMA. Lillian Danielle Tucker, if you don't get yourself together you can get up out this house! And I mean that. I'm not having it!

LILLIAN. We're going! Lil' Mama, call Junior.

LIL' MAMA. Mama?

NELLY. That didn't take long at all.

LILLIAN. Would you shut the fuck up!

MAMA. LILLIAN! What is wrong with you?

LILLIAN. *(Beside herself.)* THIS! This this this! All of it! All of this is wrong! How don't you see it, Mama? You sick and don't nobody care about it, you don't care about it. Sick over this house you can't afford to keep and don't no one want to live in. Sick over all this food for all these people same people every year and can't never afford to feed them. Bout to be feeding another mouth you can't afford and barely affording/ the one you feeding now!

(**NELLY** *seizes up.*)

MAMA. What's that mean?

Another mouth I can't afford.

What's that mean?

LILLIAN. I—

Nothing... doesn't mean nothing.

I'm just—I'm just overwhelmed and I need to go. I need to go.

(**MAMA** *looks back and forth between* **LILLIAN** *and* **NELLY**.)

MAMA. *(Quietly.)* Somebody better speak up. And fast.

(*Silence.*)

LILLIAN. *(To* **NELLY**.) You might as well tell her.

MAMA. Tell me what.

(*No one says anything.*)

LILLIAN. *(Sighing.)* Fine. Nelly's preg–

(*Before* **LILLIAN** *can finish the word,* **NELLY** *hurls a glass bottle of hot sauce directly at her. She misses only because* **LILLIAN** *ducks in time. The bottle hits the wall behind her head and shatters, leaving a stain.* **NELLY** *stares* **LILLIAN** *down; there is murder in her eyes.*)

NELLY. And Lillian is fucking a man that isn't her husband. So that's why he won't be joining us this evening.

(*No one moves. Finally,* **NELLY** *exits up the stairs. A door slams. That damn dog barks. Then* **LILLIAN**, *all of a sudden very aware of the room:*)

LILLIAN. *(To* **LIL' MAMA**.) Get upstairs!

(**LIL' MAMA**, *who has been nearly frozen watching, runs upstairs.*)

(*A minute passes or a hundred years. After a long while:*)

I left.

I didn't have nowhere else to take the kids, Mama.

I—I should've told you.

(More silence.)

You gonna take his side, fine.

(Very quiet.)

I was dying in that house, Mama. Every morning, I woke up feeling like all the life rushed out my body while I was sleep. I couldn't – Mama, I couldn't... You know, he stopped talking to me? He wouldn't look at me, touch me. Do you hear me, Mama? My husband has barely touched me/ in –

MAMA. I don't want to hear this.

LILLIAN. I was losing my mind, Mama. I don't know what happened to us, or when it did. I don't know what I did, cause we were on our way. We were really building something together and then he... he just hit a wall. Walked right into a wall nobody can see but him. And I'm watching him run into that same wall every day for ten years. I'm telling him, it's all in your head, baby. There's nothing there, it's all in your head, there's no wall. But he doesn't hear me. Soon, he don't even care to get on the other side of it, he just wanna prove everyone it's real.

I didn't think it would be easy. That's what you said. You said loving one of ours is no kind of easy. You said that. But I still did. I loved him and I gave him two children and I made him a home. I loved him all the blood out of me. All the fight I had, I spent it on him. Hell, it got to the point I didn't even care if there was anything left of me or not.

And then. And then... I met someone who saw that I needed touching. He... touched me and the color came back to my skin. He touched me and I could see in front of my face further than five minutes. I could see myself and I liked myself and I remembered myself. And I—I touched back.

(Pause.)

Well. Say what you're going to say, Mama. Just stop standing there looking/ like I –

MAMA. The rice is done. Cut off the fire.

> (**MAMA** *exits to the front of the house.* **LILLIAN** *is alone in the kitchen.)*

LILLIAN. *(Sinking.)* Oh boy. Oh boy oh boy oh boy.

Scene Five

(Later in the Tucker kitchen.)

(Everything is where we have left it. A gross, brown stain hangs on the kitchen wall where the bottle cracked earlier. The same stain that has always been there. **LIL' MAMA** *is alone, sweeping the floor.)*

*(***NELLY*** enters.)*

NELLY. Where is she?

LIL' MAMA. I don't know.

NELLY. She left?

LIL' MAMA. I don't know.

NELLY. You should have shoes on.

LIL' MAMA. I already swept there.

NELLY. Doesn't matter. It was glass.

LIL' MAMA. I know it was glass.

NELLY. Move.

> *(***NELLY*** takes the broom and nudges **LIL' MAMA** out of the way. **LIL' MAMA** watches. **NELLY** picks up a big hunk of glass and holds it for **LIL' MAMA** to see. She doesn't respond. After a while:)*

LIL' MAMA. What you gonna name it?

NELLY. ...

I don't know. If it's a boy, after his father, I guess.

LIL' MAMA. Why?

NELLY. *Why?*

LIL' MAMA. Why not name it after yourself or somethin' else?

NELLY. Cause that's not what you do.

LIL' MAMA. That's not what *who* do?

NELLY. We do. It's not what *we* do.

> *(Pause.)*

LIL' MAMA. You love him?

NELLY. Of course I love him.

LIL' MAMA. He love you?

NELLY. Yes, he loves me.

LIL' MAMA. For how long?

NELLY. What you mean, for how long? Since we been together.

LIL' MAMA. No, I mean, like, until when?

NELLY. Until... forever.

LIL' MAMA. Seems... temporary.

Seem like it run out.

NELLY. What?

> *(Pause.)*

LIL' MAMA. Mama stopped loving daddy and then daddy stopped loving mama and then mama started loving someone else.

NELLY. You shouldn't be thinking about that, Lil'/ Mama –

LIL' MAMA. I wonder when they stop loving us if it's gonna be me first or Junior. Junior act up, but mama says I don't listen and I get on her last nerve.

NELLY. That's not how it works.

LIL' MAMA. Says who?

(MAMA *enters.*)

MAMA. Lil' Mama, that hair ain't coming out them pins by itself.

LIL' MAMA. I was cleaning the/ floor.

MAMA. Nelly will finish that.

(LIL' MAMA *exits.* NELLY *resumes sweeping. Beat.*)

That wall is ruined.

NELLY. I can bleach it.

MAMA. Bleach won't do nothing but make it worse. Red like that stain brown.

(*Silence.*)

You put the rice up?

NELLY. Lil must've.

(*Pause.*)

Stew done?

MAMA. Not yet.

NELLY. Smell good.

(NELLY *takes out a spoon and tastes the stew.*)

MAMA. Not ready. Won't hardly have enough time to get ready before it's too late.

NELLY. Taste good to me.

MAMA. *(Snappy.)* Ain't about being good. About being ready. Don't take all this time to just get good.

> *(Beat.)*

NELLY. Mama—

MAMA. If you gonna fix your mouth to lie to me, you might as well keep it shut.

NELLY. You don't ever let me talk.

MAMA. What could you possibly have to say?

NELLY. I'm scared?

> *(Pause.)*

MAMA. Well. That's no excuse.

NELLY. I'm not making an excuse.

I mean, wasn't you?

MAMA. What?

NELLY. Wasn't you/ scared?

MAMA. *(A correction.)* "Weren't."

NELLY. *(Defeated.)* Okay.

> *(Beat.)*

MAMA. *(Re the dumplings.)* Come here help with this.

> *(**NELLY** crosses to do so, but not before **MAMA** sends her to wash her hands. **MAMA** starts to form the dumplings from the dough left on the counter. They work together quietly for a while.)*

> *(**MAMA** gestures to **NELLY**'s stomach.)*

How far?

NELLY. A month or so. A little more.

MAMA. A little more?

NELLY. Eight weeks. Almost nine.

MAMA. You been to a doctor?

NELLY. Yeah.

MAMA. It's healthy?

NELLY. Yeah.

MAMA. Hmmm.

> *(Beat.)*

NELLY. *(After some time.)* Mama,

I'm not...

I'm not sure I want—

> *(**MAMA** pauses her work for a moment. Waits for **NELLY** to finish, but she won't. A decision.)*

MAMA. You tell that young man come by here.

NELLY. Mama?

MAMA. You tell him to come by here and have himself put together when he comes.

NELLY. Mama, I/ have to –

> *(**MAMA** shakes her head no.)*

MAMA. You will be going to school until you can't walk and you will go back as soon as you can.

NELLY. But, Mama, I don't think I/ can [keep] –

MAMA. And you will be living here, you/ will not be staying with him in I don't// know where.

NELLY. Let me say it, Mama.

//Let me say it, Mama.

please.

(**MAMA** *stops what she's doing, looks at* **NELLY**, *really looks at her for the first time. What she sees scares her.*)

MAMA. *(Breaking.)* You are still mine, you understand?

You are still mine.

(**NELLY** *nods.* **MAMA** *is quiet, does not know how to move forward. The moment has thrown her; stunned her even. Before anything else is said,* **LIL' MAMA** *enters from upstairs, dragging her feet. Her hair is released from the scarf. She wears a fine black dress.*)

MAMA. Well, look at little miss thang here. Come all the way down the steps let me see.

(**LIL' MAMA** *reluctantly makes her way into the kitchen.*)

So it *does* fit.

LIL' MAMA. Itchy.

MAMA. Do a little twirl.

(**LIL' MAMA** *does.*)

Now that's something.

LIL' MAMA. I don't like it.

MAMA. I made that dress, you know. Had a feeling it would fit you.

LIL' MAMA. Looks old. Feels old too.

(**MAMA** *laughs.*)

MAMA. You don't know the half.

C'mere, learn something about this.

(LIL' MAMA crosses to the counter where MAMA and NELLY have been at work, but not before MAMA sends her to wash her hands.)

(To NELLY, re the dumplings) I like the way you do them. They look good how you do them.

(Having washed her hands, LIL' MAMA returns to the counter with an excessive amount of paper towels. Before she is able to dry her hands, MAMA, deeply alarmed by such a wasteful act, stops LIL' MAMA in her tracks, recovers the almost-sullied towels, rips LIL' MAMA one square with which to dry her hands, and restores the rest to their proper place in the kitchen.)

NELLY. *(To LIL' MAMA.)* Roll up your sleeves at least.

MAMA. So. You take a bit of dough and roll it into a little ball. Like this.

Do that 'til ain't no more dough left.

LIL' MAMA. When they go in?

MAMA. Last.

What you're waiting on is layers. Each layer to settle down and the next one to stack on top of the one before it. And season! You can't just wait 'til the end of it all and expect it to come out alright. You have to taste your food. And talk to your food. Every step of the way.

LIL' MAMA. Talk to the food?

MAMA. Mmmhmm. That's the trade secret.

And your fire, of course.

You have to keep a close eye on your fire

Starts out real hot and by the end it's just a flicker should keep the whole thing going.

I've been making this stew since the beginning of time. Almost like I was made to make this stew.

LIL' MAMA. What's it called?

MAMA. Don't got no name.

(On second thought.)

It's just "Stew For A Very Special Occasion."

LIL' MAMA. What's the occasion?

MAMA. A very special one.

LIL' MAMA. Like?

NELLY. Do you stop asking questions?

> *(***LILLIAN*** at the top of the stairs.* **MAMA** *sees her first.)*

MAMA. *(To* **LIL' MAMA.***)* Go upstairs so you can change out of that and we can steam it.

> *(To* **NELLY.***)*

You, too. Go get dressed.

> *(***NELLY*** heads up the stairs with* **LIL' MAMA,** *passing* **LILLIAN** *on the way. It's tense between them for the brief moment that they pass on the stairs.* **LILLIAN** *descends.)*

LILLIAN. Junior back yet?

MAMA. Hasn't come in since I been down here.

LILLIAN. Well, we waiting on him. Soon as he's back, we'll be leaving.

MAMA. If that's what you want.

LILLIAN. We'll still help carry the things over to the church and show face. We'll just leave from there.

MAMA. If that's what you want.

LILLIAN. Well, yeah. I think it's best.

MAMA. I haven't asked you to go. You could stay.

LILLIAN. I don't think that's a good idea, Mama.

MAMA. *(Disappointed.)* Well, you know best.

LILLIAN. I gotta... figure this out, you know?

MAMA. *(Struggling to wrap her mouth around these words.)* You gonna go see [about that man]?

LILLIAN. I'm going home. I have to go home, right?

MAMA. I don't know why you asking me.

LILLIAN. *(Scoffs.)* Right.

MAMA. Well, what do you want me to say?

LILLIAN. Anything? Tell me what to do? Tell me what not to do? I don't know.

Nothing.

Never mind.

> *(Beat.)*

MAMA. I almost left. Once.

LILLIAN. ... You never told me that.

MAMA. Some things you just don't tell.

> *(As **MAMA** talks, she puts the kettle to boil.)*

It got to a point between us, actually, I was right around your age, where I'd come home from teaching and every night felt exactly the same. I'd start dinner and wait for him and he'd come home and wait for me to finish. And we'd eat and I'd wait for him to tell me about his day.

Most days he would say little and one day he stopped saying much of anything at all. I'd pour him his nightcap and go upstairs waiting for him to come to bed. Some nights he would. Most nights he wouldn't. And it went on like that for what felt like a lifetime, me waiting on him. And I just got tired of it. Until one day I wasn't tired any more, I was angry. I realized that all that time I wasn't waiting on him, I was waiting on me.

LILLIAN. Waiting on you?

MAMA. Waiting on me to do some different. Felt like my life was what it was, like it was chosen for me. And all of a sudden, I wanted to get in the way of it. I wanted to turn it all over. And I did. One of those nights I packed my bag and got in the car before he got home. And I just drove. Just got on the highway and drove. No idea where I was going. Was on the road nearly four hours 'fore it occurred to me I was driving to my mama's house. Only place I knew to go, I guess. And, hell, by the time I got here I was more afraid of what she'd think of what I'd done than what I actually did.

LILLIAN. I was there that/ summer.

MAMA. that summer. Yes, you were.

And your brother. He was—

He was with us then too.

LILLIAN. You're okay.

MAMA. Yes, I know. It just—

LILLIAN. comes and goes.

MAMA. Yes.

(Quiet. The women remember.)

LILLIAN. Was she was mad at you?

MAMA. Who?

LILLIAN. Your mother.

MAMA. No.

LILLIAN. Disappointed?

(MAMA *shakes her head.*)

MAMA. I think she was scared for me, more than anything. And frustrated she couldn't fix it. So she did what she could do.

LILLIAN. What's that?

MAMA. She fed me. Cooked so much food almost had to roll me back to your daddy.

(MAMA *chuckles. Pause.*)

LILLIAN. (*A disappointment.*) You stayed.

MAMA. (*That stung.*) I did.

But I'd be lying if I said there weren't more days than not I don't wonder what would've happened if I didn't.

(LILLIAN *and* MAMA *lock eyes.* MAMA *goes back to gathering fixings for her tea. Cream. Two sugars. A little bit of cinnamon.*)

LILLIAN. When did you know?

MAMA. Know what?

LILLIAN. That none of it would go the way you planned?

(MAMA *thinks about this awhile. Smiles.*)

MAMA. When you popped out my pussy at seventeen.

LILLIAN. Mama!

MAMA. You popped out my pussy and looked me dead in the eye and said "we doing this?" And I said, "I guess we are."

LILLIAN. I didn't know you said pussy.

MAMA. I say pussy. Pussy! And, after a day like today, I'm saying shit and damn and fuck too.

Shit! Damn!

Fuck!

> (**MAMA** *and* **LILLIAN** *laugh out loud until it hurts. Or until it stops hurting. If there's a difference. Eventually, it settles.*)

LILLIAN. I'm gonna finish putting myself together. You coming?

MAMA. I'll have my tea and be up right behind you.

LILLIAN. You let me know when Junior gets here.

> (**LILLIAN** *starts up the stairs. She walks slowly, takes her time.*)

MAMA. Do you think it's enough?

LILLIAN. There's more than enough.

MAMA. No, I just... you sometimes wonder if it was enough, you know. If you could've... that maybe you could've done more for your...

LILLIAN. *(A gentle stop.)* Mm-mm.

MAMA. And, if you did, could you maybe have stopped... uh, this or that from—you know? You just keep, you know, going over it and over it/ all.

LILLIAN. Hey.

MAMA. Hmmm?

LILLIAN. *(Tender.)* That's all in your head. Yeah?

It's all in your head.

> (**MAMA** *nods.* **LILLIAN** *continues up the stairs.*)

> (**MAMA** *takes in the kitchen. All of her work. Takes in the day. All of her work. She takes a deep deep breath in. She turns on her tabletop radio: Gospel, again (she likes what*

> *she likes). For what it's worth, she is at peace,*
> *interrupted only in the slightest by that*
> *tireless dog barking somewhere in the near*
> *distance.)*

MAMA. *(To herself.)* Imma kill that dog. I swear to God I am.

> *(MAMA goes to the cupboard, pulls out her*
> *mug.)*

Imma kill it, Imma cut it up, and Imma cook it.

> *(The gentle ding of a timer. The kettle steams.)*

(To the kettle.) I'm coming, I'm coming.

> *(Then, all of a sudden:)*

> *(A loud, popping noise from somewhere near.)*

What was that—?!

> *(MAMA, jumping at the sound of the noise,*
> *accidentally knocks over her cup of tea, which*
> *shatters upon hitting the floor. She stares at*
> *the shattered cup. It bewilders her.)*

> *(The dog barks madly outside.)*

(As if someone might answer.) What *was* that?

> *(To herself, to the room.)*

I don't know –

What was that... what was that sound?

Don't know... Someone's tire probably.

Someone's tire?

Yes, someone's/ [tire].

LIL' MAMA. What was that?

(**LIL' MAMA** *appears in her bedclothes and a satin scarf. She heads toward the back window directly to where* **MAMA** *stands and with such intention that* **MAMA** *moves out of her way.*)

(*There is something different about her. She is economic in her movement and speech. She does not address* **MAMA**. *Instead, she speaks as if she were the only one present in the room. As much as possible, her speech should be continuous.*)

MAMA. Oh! You startled/ me.

LIL' MAMA. I thought I heard...

MAMA. It was/ just someone's tire.

LIL' MAMA. It was outside?

MAMA. Let it alone.

LIL' MAMA. Where's Junior?

(*Without looking at* **MAMA**, **LIL' MAMA** *heads out the back door searching for the answer herself.* **MAMA** *tries her best to prevent her from leaving, but before she can stop her,* **NELLY** *has arrived in the kitchen. She, too, speaks as if she was the only one present in the room. Somewhere in here, the steaming kettle begins to whistle.*)

MAMA. He'll be back/ soon.

NELLY. What happened?

MAMA. Let it alone.

NELLY. I heard a [pop] –

MAMA. It was just/ someone's tire.

NELLY. But tires blow, they don't pop like that.

MAMA. Well, that's what it/ was.

NELLY. Where's Junior?

MAMA. He'll be back/ soon.

> (*Like* LIL' MAMA, NELLY *exits out the back door without acknowledging* MAMA. *Again,* MAMA *is unable to stop her in time. Just as she is reaching for* NELLY, LILLIAN *arrives in the kitchen, moving and speaking with no regard for* MAMA.)

LILLIAN. What was that/?

I thought I heard –

MAMA. It was – someone's tire/ blew out.

LILLIAN. I'm not sure/.

MAMA. I'm sure. I was down here.

> (*Unsure.*)

Wasn't/ I?

LILLIAN. It almost sounded/ like [a]

MAMA. It was just/ someone's tire.

LILLIAN. And where is Junior?

MAMA. He –

> (LILLIAN *finally turns and looks at* MAMA. *She looks at* MAMA *as if she is expecting an answer. It makes* MAMA *dizzy.* MAMA *tries to answer, but the words are caught somewhere way before her throat.* LILLIAN *will remain this way, trained on* MAMA, *for as long as she must, waiting for her answer. When she is ready, she, too, goes to see about the trouble outside.* MAMA *is left alone in the kitchen.*)

(*Soon after* **LILLIAN**'s *exit, we hear a woman's dreadful wailing just beyond the back door. As if there was a sound assigned to someone splitting in two. The dog barks madly. The kettle shrieks. The woman screams and screams and screams.*)

(*The wailing evolves (maybe there are more voices), encroaching further on the kitchen. It becomes the shrieking kettle, the howling dog, the choir crescendo, all of a sudden much louder than it was, beaming from the tabletop radio. At a point, it may be difficult to discern whether the sounds come from within the walls or without. It is difficult for* **MAMA** *as well. It paralyzes her. It threatens to floor her. She rocks unto herself.*)

(*At some point, however, she will find within it all the sweet, sweet sound from earlier. We will find it with her. Remember? This is the day. Perhaps she begins by humming a few notes, singing a few choice lines. Through it, she tries to regain her balance, steady herself. She makes it to the door. Shuts it. She makes it to the kettle. Turns it off. The wailing begins to fade until, eventually, all of the sounds that had just overwhelmed the space restore to the natural sounds of the here and now: something is cooking down on the stove, a dog barks outside, the tabletop radio plays.*)

(*And so smoothly so that we won't be able to say when exactly it happened, but it did. The sound carried us back, carried* **MAMA** *over.*)

(**MAMA** *makes her way to the stove. Turns off the kettle. She returns to the stew. Picks up a spoon. Stirs. Tastes. Adds this and that.*

Adjusts the fire. She knows the stew. She needs it. The stew is unchanging. The stew will fill the space. It will heal. It must. It must.)

(The lights dim on the kitchen. MAMA *will tend to the stew even when its dark.)*

End of Play

Printed in the USA
CPSIA information can be obtained
at www.ICGtesting.com
LVHW020616250823
756160LV00003B/95